My Story
Viking Blood

Andrew D

"And now, your journey must begin, God of Thunder! Many undreamed of dangers await thee, but you are armed with truth, and your own awesome strength! You must not falter."

"Journey into Mystery with The Mighty Thor" #118
Stan Lee/Jack Kirby

While the events described and some of the characters in this book may be based on actual historical events and real people, Tor Scaldbane is a fictional character, created by the author, and his story is a work of fiction.

Scholastic Children's Books,
Euston House, 24 Eversholt Street,
London NW1 1DB, UK

A division of Scholastic Ltd
London ~ New York ~ Toronto ~ Sydney ~ Auckland
Mexico City ~ New Delhi ~ Hong Kong

First published in the UK by Scholastic Ltd, 2008
This edition published by Scholastic Ltd, 2016

ISBN 978 1407 16575 2

Typeset by M Rules
Printed and bound in the UK by CPI Group (UK) Ltd, Croydon, CR0 4YY

2 4 6 8 10 9 7 5 3 1

Now

It was the end of my story. I knew as soon as I saw the wolf that I had been careless and that now he would rip me apart with those teeth.

I was annoyed that I had been so stupid as to wander and chance upon the hungriest beast in the forest without even a sword. I had never meant to go so far.

Old One Ear the wolf took a step closer. He must have spent the rest of the winter hiding in the deep forest and now there were young lambs again he was back. Just like last year.

I was in the middle of the clearing and had nowhere to run. I moved my wooden rune staff so that it was between my body and the wolf, and I held it tightly in my hand.

I thought of Ragnar and his sword with the golden hammer, but I had left him a long way behind by the waterfall.

I knew that One Ear would surely kill me and eat me right there. If only to stop me raising the alarm. If only because he hadn't been able to sink his sharp, glistening fangs into my flesh on that terrible day back in the frozen mid-winter when he hunted me and Magnus in this same forest.

One Ear shifted his head from side to side. As he moved, I saw that there was something very wrong with his left eye. It was an old wound about an inch across and flesh had healed over the eye, leaving it dead and useless. I wondered if he remembered me.

The wolf curved his old body, keeping his good eye fixed firmly on me. It was a hunting movement, and it reminded me that I was about to be eaten alive. If I turned and broke into a run, I knew the wolf would be on me and bring me down in seconds. I was a long way from the village or help.

I wanted to fight like Thor, but I had no mighty hammer. I wanted to struggle against this beast like Odin fighting Fenris at the end of days, but I knew that like him, I would lose.

I had no proper weapon again. I had my long staff of twisted wood, and if I could get it out in time, I had my small knife in my pocket for cutting plants. And, of course, I had just one hand to fight with. But this time I had no help.

What a pair we must have looked. Tor the Tale and Old One Ear. A boy of sixteen summers with a stump where his right hand should be, and a wolf with one ear and one eye.

Now I was near the end, I suddenly wondered what had happened to my hand, left so far away on a muddy battlefield, across the sea in another land. Had it been trampled by heavy leather boots and buried deep in mud? Or was it stripped to the bone by ravens with open-mouthed young to feed?

The old wolf took a step closer, bending his head down towards the ground. Not yet ready to leap, but nearly.

I carefully leaned the staff against my shoulder and moved my left hand towards the pocket where my knife was. I had it out now, hidden under my clothes so that it wouldn't catch the high midday sun and draw the wolf's attention.

In one quick sweep, I stepped forward and moved my staff so that it pointed towards One Ear like a blunt spear. The wolf snorted. My left hand held the knife low and out of sight. I had an idea of using the staff and stabbing with the knife, but then I saw again the size of his jaws and I knew this really was the end.

One Ear came a step forwards. I poked the staff. He moved back. Again he came forwards, and again I poked the staff towards him. He barely moved.

He was so close now that I could smell his breath. It smelt of rotting teeth, festering meat and death. It smelt like a battlefield.

His lips quivered, exposing sharp yellow daggers. His breath was heavy now. He was near the end of his life. But then, so was I now.

I suddenly got annoyed that this old wolf would be the finish of my story, instead of me being the end of his.

I saw his muscles tense up. He snarled. Then, in a burst of movement and fury, and hatred and hunger, One Ear leapt towards me…

The story of the beginning

Thirteen moons earlier…

I saw my father in the bay, but then he turned into a whale.

I was watching the ocean from my lookout point on the cliff, just where the edge of the forest meets the open ground. From this height, you could see nearly half a day's rowing out to sea.

I saw a black speck getting larger. A long black speck. It was moving towards the shore against the flow of the tide. I saw spray being splashed up as the dragon figurehead of my father's ship cut through the water on its way home. Then, as it got closer, I saw that it wasn't a ship but a whale, and the spray was from its blowhole. It was only a small whale – not even half the length of the longboat. It was probably young and probably lost.

"I told you," said Ragnar. "They're not coming today."

"They might be," I answered. But I didn't think they were.

Ragnar shook his head. "The tide's against them for one thing, and for another, it's too soon. They won't be back yet. There are too many churches with too many gold plates and silver coins on the other side of the sea."

I thought he was probably right, but I didn't tell him that. Ragnar is a whole year older than me. He is my adopted brother, although he's actually my cousin. My father and his father were brothers. When we were both small, his father went on a raiding party and didn't come back. Afterwards Ragnar came to live with us. In the village, he was the best for his age at sword fighting and wrestling. (But only because he is a year taller than me.)

"I'm…" said Ragnar, pointing downhill. I knew he meant, "I'm going to go back to the village and see if anyone wants to practise sword-fighting by the river. Are you coming?"

"No. I'll…" I said, and I pointed out to sea which meant, "No, I'll stay here for a bit and keep a watch out, but I might join you later." Most of the time we knew what the other one meant without needing to say it.

"All right. But they won't be back today."

Ragnar turned and ran down the hill towards the village. Soon the thump of his footsteps were lost in the sound of the sea crashing on the rocks below.

I narrowed my eyes and scanned the horizon carefully, but there was nothing to see except low, grey cloud hanging close to the water. There were no masts appearing over the horizon. There were no longboats being rowed into view.

My father had been away for nearly a whole moon. He sailed on a raiding ship with nine other men from the village. The ship called at villages along the coast and took the best fighting men from each of them. My father is the chieftain of our village and he is always chosen.

Raiding is a dangerous business and it is only for the strongest warriors. The others don't last long. Some of the women don't like the men leaving at all and would rather they stay on their farms all summer, tending to the animals and growing crops.

I was nearly fifteen summers old and next time my father went on a raiding voyage he would take me with him. I was ready. More than anything I wanted to go and fight and be a warrior.

If a warrior dies honourably in battle then he goes straight to Valhalla to feast alongside Odin, king of the gods. Not that I want to die. But great warriors also have songs and poems and stories told about them. Stories that people tell and tell again and are never forgotten. They last forever, just like the stories about the gods.

People called me Tor the Voice, probably because they thought I talked a lot, even though I didn't. People used to call me Tor the Question, but I didn't like it and now they don't. I wanted to be called Tor the Sword. Or maybe Tor the Bloody, except that people might have thought I slaughtered cattle for a trade, like Sigund the Bloody. So I thought Tor the Sword would be best.

From up at my lookout point, I could see almost everything. The cliff ended in a sheer drop into the sea below, while in the other direction the land descended in a steep incline to the cattle pastures and then the buildings. Not only could you spot any ships approaching out to sea, but you could also see over almost the whole village. The only thing you couldn't see was Olaf the blacksmith's forge beyond the tree line, but you could always tell where it was from the smoke that rose through his roof when he was working.

You could see Asgot the Green building a wall from rocks, carefully choosing each stone to fit the next gap. You could see three slaves sowing barley in a field. And in the middle of the afternoon, you could see Harald the Thread's wife, Gudrid, sneak away from her washing duty at the river, walk round the edge of the village and duck into the woods. At the same time on the other side of the village, Sigund the Bloody would leave the cows he was supposed to be tending and also disappear into the woods. I was sure they didn't realize that from up there you could see almost everything.

Just then I heard voices from the forest just near me. Figures flickered in and out of view as they moved against the trees. A black shape flapped down from a tree branch and made me jump.

"CAW!"

It was Flagg the Raven. He was not a warrior who wore black feathers to frighten his enemies on the battlefield. He actually was a raven.

"CAW! CAW!"

Then I saw Magnus. He is known as Magnus the Tale. Or Magnus the Old. Olaf the blacksmith once told me that Magnus was over one hundred years old, but I didn't think that could be true because no one could live that long except the gods.

Magnus lives in a hut halfway between the village and where the proper forest begins. People go to him when they are ill, or when they want him to throw crow bones to see what will happen in the future. Girls go to him to see who they are going to marry. He knows all about the Old Ways and the Old Gods. And most of all, he knows stories. So many stories.

"Magnus!" I called to him.

Coming along behind Magnus was Sven the Silent. Some people call him Sven the Stupid behind his back. As usual he had an armful of leaves and herbs from the forest. He was always grinding plants and cooking up potions.

Magnus smiled as he walked up to me. Flagg hopped ahead of him, one wing longer than the other. Magnus found the raven in the forest as a fledgling with a broken wing, and now the bird never strayed far from his side.

Sven the Silent walked past me with just the smallest nod of recognition and continued downhill towards the village without even breaking his stride.

Magnus looked at me, then out to sea, then back at me again.

"They're not coming home today," he said.

"I know," I said. "I know that. For a start the tide is against them, and anyway, they haven't been away long enough."

"Your father will be all right though. Don't worry about him."

My stomach suddenly felt sick. Until that second I hadn't even considered that my father might not return. I'd been training with a sword, and swimming, and learning to handle sails on a ship in the bay, all to prepare for when he took me with him next time.

"Tor?"

What if he were killed? What would happen then?

"Tor? Are you all right?"

"CAW!"

Black wings fluttered just in front of my face.

"Who me? Of course I'm all right. Just thinking about all the people my father must be killing on the battlefield," I said.

Magnus made a sour-looking face. I don't know why.

"What have you been doing?" I asked, to change the subject.

"Asgot the Green has a slave with a swollen foot," said Magnus. "And in his field, he has a goat that won't give birth even though it's more than her time."

We walked along the top of the cliff together for a while, not really saying anything. Magnus always knew what was happening. He was always looking at the sea or at birds or the sky, and then suddenly he'd tell you something that always came true. Like if there was going to be a storm or when the birds on the cliffs would be laying their eggs for the second batch of chicks.

"Are you sure that my father will come back?" I said it without looking at his face.

Magnus paused and so did I.

"There are many perils when a man goes raiding. Firstly, there's the sea crossing itself. Away from the safety of the coast, there's the danger of strong winds ripping the sails apart or snapping the mast. Or a sudden storm sinking the ship far, far from any land, and men drowning in a cold, rough sea."

He wasn't making me feel any better, and I was sorry I'd asked the question. But he carried on regardless.

"If they cross the sea safely, there is the risk of being seen approaching and that the alarm will be raised. Or that people will be ready for a raid and prepared for battle with superior forces. Or perhaps the landing goes wrong because the tide or weather is against you. Or maybe the raid will fail because of accidents and the battle will be lost. But," he said, raising a finger, "but I am sure your father will return. He still believes in the Old Ways. Wise and cunning Odin will watch over him and see him safely back to you."

I felt so much better when Magnus said the last bit. Odin is my father's favourite god. The god of war and wisdom and poetry. The chief god and in charge of Asgard, the home of the gods, just like my father is in charge of our village.

"It's an old boat as well. It has sailed that journey many times and it knows the way home."

Once a ship has sailed to a place several times, the spirit of the ship begins to remember the route so you are more likely to get home safely.

Magnus and I walked on further, with Flagg hopping and half flying ahead of us. We kept going until we came to where the rocks curved and you could see mountains stretching out inland. If you looked straight at them, their brilliant white peaks were nearly blinding in the sun. Fire and ice.

I suddenly realized we hadn't arrived at this place by accident.

Burning yellow sun in the sky. White snow on the mountains.

Fire and ice.

"So," said Magnus, as if he'd been waiting our entire conversation to get to this point, "I hear that you are somewhat muddled about the creation of the world."

"No," I said, rather stupidly.

Three days before, after swimming, one of the children in the village had asked me to tell them the story of how the world was created. I didn't do it very well.

"I'm all right on the beginning and the end," I admitted. "But I got muddled up in the middle."

"It's easily done," said Magnus, which made me feel better. "Especially if you are simple minded," he added, which didn't.

Magnus sat down on the grass and I settled next to him.

"Hail to the speaker and hail to the listener. May whoever hears and learns these words prosper because of them. Hail to those who listen," intoned Magnus.

He always says that at the beginning of a story. I think it is his way of getting your attention. It may have been my imagination, but I'm sure he put a bit of extra emphasis on "those who listen", which was a bit uncalled for.

"In the beginning," he boomed loudly, "there were only two things…"

He pointed to the sky, where the sun was blazing, warming our faces.

"Fire!" I said.

"And…"

He pointed to the mountains where the snow lay still and silent.

"Ice!"

"In the beginning there were only two things – fire and ice. The ice and snow were in the north, and the fire and smoke were in the south. And in between these two elements was a great void of…"

"Nothing," I offered. (Which I knew was right.)

"The north part of the void was freezing and the south

part of the void was boiling. Somewhere in the middle was life. It woke up, and then stood, and then stretched, and was a giant called Ymir. Ymir began to sweat and the drops of his sweat became a man and a woman, the very first frost giants."

Magnus inflated his scrawny old chest, puffing it out as large as he could to portray a frost giant, all sharp fangs, and icicles, and hatred. Even if Magnus wasn't one hundred years old, his bony chest certainly looked it through his shirt.

"Then another creature emerged from the void of nothing. It was a giant cow. Rivers of milk flowed from her underside and fed the frost giants. She licked the ice in the north, and part of the ice began to move and breathe, and this was Buri, the very first god. Time beyond measure came and went, and soon Buri had three powerful grandsons – Odin, Vili and Ve. And this of course was our own Odin who keeps us safe today."

I thought of the sacrifices that father made to Odin before he sailed, and I hoped the god was watching over him.

"There was no day and no night, for they did not exist yet, but time still found a way of passing because without time there is no story. Now, the three brothers began to hate the frost giants with a deep passion that filled their minds. They decided to hide in the swirling mist deep in the forest and lie in wait for Ymir. When he neared, they jumped out and killed him in a terrible fight. The three brothers used

Ymir's corpse to create all that we see," said Magnus, pointing around him.

"His body they made into the earth we stand on," said Magnus stamping his feet. "And his bones became the mountains. His teeth became rocks. There was so much blood from his wounds that it flowed in a giant river and became the sea. The brothers hollowed out Ymir's skull and lifted it into place where it remains today as the sky. They scooped pieces of brain out of the skull and threw them high into the sky, where they became clouds."

There were no clouds above us just now so I guessed Ymir didn't have quite enough brains to go round.

"And that is how our world, 'Midgard', was made," finished Magnus the Tale.

"What about people?" I said. "What about us?"

"Walking through the world, the brothers found two trees that had fallen to the ground. One was an elm and the other was an ash. The brothers took the fallen trees and breathed a spark of life into them, making a man called Ask and a woman called Embla. All people, in all lands, are the offspring of these two, the first humans."

"Even us?"

"Certainly. The brothers then created a land called Jotunheim for the frost giants and rock giants to live in. But because the giants were so strong, so dangerous, and worst of all, so angry, the brothers did not trust such ugly creatures. So they enclosed the realm of the giants using Ymir's eyebrows to create a range of tall mountains."

Magnus pointed to the distant mountains again.

"Caw!"

Flagg started hopping about for absolutely no reason. Perhaps he had fleas.

"And what about a home for the gods?"

"For themselves, the gods created Asgard, a city high above the world. And for when the gods wanted to visit earth (or if they wished to visit the land of the giants to bash their skulls) they made a long bridge that was all the colours of the rainbow, and they called that Bifrost, the flaming bridge."

"CAW!"

Flagg was fidgeting. He suddenly flapped his one and a half wings and flew off in an awkward zigzag flight. He always looked as if he'd fly into a tree at any moment, but he never did.

I ignored the raven. This was my favourite part of the story. I interlocked the fingers of both my hands and wiggled them around.

"The maggots," smiled Magnus. "And where do they come from?"

"Later on," I said quickly, "Odin and his brothers remembered the slimy yellow maggots that had hatched in Ymir's dead flesh after they had killed him. They took the maggots and shaped them into little men who liked the dark and loved the damp, and these became the dwarfs." I wiggled my fingers again. "Made from maggots."

I looked up at Magnus. "When I'm a warrior, you'll be able to tell stories about me and the enemies I kill on the battlefield."

Magnus wasn't listening to me. He was looking towards the upper pastures where the sheep are always enclosed in the afternoon. We could both hear voices. Someone was shouting an alarm, although we could not hear what they were saying. Without speaking, we both stood up and headed in the direction of the sounds.

We reached the pasture just in time to see three men running into the forest. They were armed, one of them with a sword and the other two with bows and arrows. The men leapt over the undergrowth and disappeared into the trees.

On the far side of the pasture I saw why. There was a sheep covered in blood lying on its side. Its neck had been ripped out and so had its stomach. Red intestines streaked with grey trailed across the clean green grass.

"Old One Ear," said Magnus.

Old One Ear was a large, lone male wolf that lived in the forest. He preyed on our animals and was the bane of our farmers' lives. Some people said he was mad. Others said he could change shape to sneak up on prey and to escape being hunted afterwards.

A few years ago, one of our men had got close enough to him to take off most of his left ear with a sword. When a search party found the man's body a few days later, most of his flesh had been eaten. Whoever finally killed the wolf would certainly get a story told in their honour.

Flagg hopped on to the dead sheep's head and begun pecking at its eye. I felt a bit sick watching him do it.

Magnus went over to the sheep. I thought he was going to stop Flagg, but instead he whispered something about Odin. Then he reached down, dug his fingers into the sheep's eye socket and plucked out a soggy orb. He threw it on the grass for Flagg to eat more easily.

"Caw!"

"We'd better take it down to the village," said Magnus.

He was right of course. Now that it was dead, the sheep couldn't be wasted. They would skin the body for a winter coat and then spit-roast the rest for food. I didn't think Magnus was strong enough to carry it all the way down to the village, but he was keen to try.

As I got closer, the smell of the open guts hit me.

"Ugh!"

"Come on, it's not too bad," said Magnus.

I leant down to pick up the rear end of the sheep and as I did the smell hit me again, but worse. I doubled over and threw up. Warm vomit splashed over my shoes and left bits in my mouth. I spat them out.

Magnus looked at me and frowned. "You'll see a lot worse than that in battle."

One of the men came back from the forest.

"The wolf is well away. We didn't even catch sight of him," he reported.

Flagg had finished eating his eyeball and took flight, zigzagging down the hill.

"Come on, take the other end," said the man.

At first I thought he was talking to Magnus, but then I realized he meant me. I wiped the vomit away from the side of my mouth and grabbed hold of the sheep's rear legs.

I held my breath all the way down the hill as Magnus's last words went round and round in my head.

The story of the hammer

"Will you keep it steady!" shouted Olaf, expelling a large gob of spit from the corner of his mouth.

I was standing in the workshop of Olaf the Smith, pumping the bellows for him while he worked. Olaf the Smith worked with iron, tin, silver and gold. The hut was full of smoke and fumes and steam from the fire. It was hard not to cough. There was a hole in the roof to let the smoke out, but the smoke didn't seem to know that.

"Just keep it steady, Tor," said Olaf again, much quieter this time. Sometimes I thought Olaf would like to shout at me more than he did.

"I am," I said.

I felt a trickle of sweat run down my back. The fire was very hot and I had to be really close to it to work.

"That's it, keep it regular," said Olaf, encouraging me.

The bellows are sort of bags that you push down on. They blow air into the fire and make it hotter. That is why you have to keep them going at a regular rate, so that the fire doesn't get too hot or too cool.

I was only in Olaf's forge because my mother had sent me

with a broken bread pan for Olaf to mend. There was still no word of my father or any sign of his longship returning from across the sea. I had watched from my lookout point again that morning, for as long as I could.

Olaf's proper assistant went outside for a while because the smoke had made his chest hurt again, so Olaf put me on the bellows instead.

I didn't mind. I liked to see Olaf work.

Olaf took whatever metal he was working on, heated it in the fire until it was red hot, removed it with his tongs, and then beat and twisted it into whatever shape he wanted on the anvil.

He made most of the weapons for the entire village. He never went away in a longship to go raiding. My father said his skills were too valuable to risk losing.

In the corner of the hut was a pile of long wooden poles. Olaf would add a sharp metal head to each of them, then they would become spears to throw on the battlefield. Next to them was another pile of shorter, thicker wooden poles that, with a strong blade, would become battle-axes. The far side of the hut was full of iron helmets, arrowheads, shields and, best of all, swords. All of them neatly ordered by type and strength so Olaf could find exactly what any person wanted. One day Olaf would make me a sword of my own.

"How many weapons do you think you've made in your life?" I asked. Olaf was quite old. He'd probably seen more than fifty summers.

"Many," said Olaf.

He didn't look up at me at all, but kept his concentration on bringing his hammer smashing down on the sword blade he'd just heated, sending orange sparks flying through the air. He reminded me of a dwarf hammering away at a dark magical forge under the mountains.

"I'm sure my swords and axes have killed many men on the battlefield and in drunken arguments. Good men and bad men," he added. "But I don't just make weapons. My horseshoes have carried many husbands back to wives, my plates have held many feasts, and my hammers have built many fences and farms." Olaf wasn't much of a joker.

He also made all the nails and the metal joinings for the new longship the men were building in the next bay.

"One day, I'm sure one of the swords I've made will kill that wolf," said Olaf.

I imagined a sword in my hand doing just that. Killing the wolf.

"The men are taking goats up to the pasture today to set a trap for Old One Ear," I said.

"I know. They won't catch him. He's far too cunning for that. His time hasn't come yet," answered Olaf, with a calm certainty in his voice that made me believe him.

There was a noise at the door and one of the slaves came into the hut with a bucket of bog ore he had dug up from the wet ground near the river. He put down the bucket and quickly disappeared again. Without breaking the rhythm of his hammering, Olaf kicked over the bucket, sending the rocks scattering across the floor to join a pile already there. Olaf would melt down these rocks in his furnace to make the iron he needed for nails.

Olaf lifted his foot and flicked the side of the empty bucket, sending it spinning into the air and then, still without looking, kicked it out through the doorway. I heard it clatter as it hit the slave boy.

"Oooff!"

Olaf finished his careful hammering and thrust the sword blade into a bucket of water, sending up a cloud of hissing steam. He waited a moment, then pulled it out and admired his own handiwork.

"Keep going!" he bellowed at me. "Nobody told you to stop. We need the fire. We always need the fire."

I kept pumping the bellows even though it was hard to keep things as regular as Olaf liked.

"I can't do any more with that blade until it's cold. Shall we make some amulets for the gods?" said Olaf, with a sudden smile that really surprised me.

"Yes!"

"I have to make some anyway, so I might as well do it while I have you to work the bellows for me," he added, slipping back into his usual grumpier self.

A lot of people like to wear amulets that represent their

favourite god. If you choose the right god and please him with worship, then they can bring you luck in battle if you're going to war or raiding, or make sure your crops grow and your animals are healthy if you're a farmer. The two most popular gods are Odin and Thor.

Odin is the chief of the gods. He is also known as the All-Father and is the ruler of Asgard, the city of the gods. Odin is the god of war and wisdom. He has two ravens that sit one on each shoulder. One of the ravens is named Hugin, which means "thought", and the other is named Munn, which means "memory". Every morning, Odin sends out his ravens to fly across all the worlds and then return to him to report all that they have seen. Nothing escapes Odin.

When I think of Odin, I picture him as a powerful old warrior, perhaps fifty or more summers old, with a thick grey beard. Odin always wears an eye patch because he had once plucked out his own eye to gain some secret knowledge that he wanted. Odin is the favourite god of people who go to war, like my father, and also of people like Magnus the Old, who seek stories and wisdom.

Olaf went over to the corner of the hut, opened a chest and took out something wrapped in a cloth. He whispered a few words to himself and then carefully unwrapped the cloth. I knew what it was before I saw it.

"We'll make a tribute to Thor," he said quietly.

Inside the cloth was a piece of grey stone that had three

holes in the shape of small hammers hollowed out of it. The hammers represented the god Thor.

"You think you can keep the fire steady?" asked Olaf.

Olaf knew that I loved the chance to make amulets or anything connected to the gods, so it wasn't really much of a question.

"Of course I can," I said, wiping sweat off my forehead so I was ready. It was really hot that close to the fire, but I had to keep going.

Thor is the most popular god in the village. He's the most popular god everywhere. My own name, Tor, was given in his honour. Thor is so popular that there are more than fifty variations of his name for boys and even some for girls.

Thor is one of Odin's many sons, and is the god of thunder and lightning. He's a great warrior, and in the stories he's always slaying giants and other enemies of Asgard with his fighting hammer called Mjollnir.

Whenever Thor travels across the sky in his chariot pulled by goats, the heavens shake with thunder. Thor has red hair, a red beard and a great hunger for ale and cooked meat. Thor can control the weather and if he's angry one day he might send a thunderstorm to sink an enemy's ship, or if he's pleased send fair weather to a goat-herder that he likes.

I looked over at Olaf and saw that he now had several small lumps of metal in his hand.

"Silver?" I asked.

"Yes, of course, silver. This is for Thor," said Olaf, his eyes fixed once more on his task.

No one knew where Olaf hid his precious metals like gold and silver, but he always seemed to have them to hand when he needed them.

Olaf put a metal vessel, shaped like a little cup, into the fire. When it was hot enough, he would add the silver to melt. Then, really carefully, he would pour the molten metal into the mould without spilling or wasting a single drop.

"My assistant is good, but he's boring," grumbled Olaf. "All day I'm in here with him working. He never says anything. If I ask him a question, he just coughs. Always coughing. But you love to talk, don't you?"

"Not really," I said, which was a bit of a lie.

"Tell me a story, and if I like it, you can pour the silver. Do you think you could do it? Carefully?"

"Yes, I'll do it. I can do it."

Pouring the metal is the most important part. He had never let me do that before. Ever.

"Do you have a story?"

I thought about what story to tell.

"Keep the bellows steady!" Olaf yelled.

I was really hot and my shirt was soaked all the way through with sweat. Thin black fumes rose from the burning charcoal in the fire. I released the bellows, letting them suck in air, then I pushed their handles together and the bellows breathed out into the fire. The charcoal crackled and glowed white, and on my skin I felt the fire get ever hotter as we got ready to make the hammers of Thor.

I knew what story I would tell…

One morning in Asgard, Thor woke very early to find that his hammer had vanished during the night. Thor's hammer, Mjollnir, was the mightiest weapon that the gods had. It kept them safe from the frost giants and the rock giants, who lived in fear that Thor would use the hammer to crack open their skulls.

Thor almost tore Asgard apart looking for the hammer, but despite a frantic search, it was nowhere to be found. The gods were worried.

"The frost giants dare not attack Asgard while we have Thor and his hammer to defend us, but without it, I fear they'll soon be banging at our gate," said Odin.

Loki agreed to help search for the hammer. Loki lived with the gods as one of them, although he was really of giant blood. Odin had killed Loki's father in battle and then adopted the baby boy as his own, and half-brother to Thor. Loki appeared to be charming, but he was cunning and evil by nature. Like Odin, he had the ability to change his shape and become an animal, like a bird, a salmon or an otter.

Knowing how important the hammer was, Loki

changed into a falcon and flew high over Asgard, but he couldn't see Thor's hammer anywhere. Then he flapped his wings and soared over Midgard, the land of men, but he could still see no sign of Mjollnir.

Loki flew on to the land of the giants and there he saw that Thrym, king of the frost giants, was looking very pleased with himself. Thrym stood as high as six tall men. He was an icy grey in colour, with hard blood-red eyes, and a mouth full of sharp pointed fangs each as long as a mortal man's fingers. He was a frightening sight and enjoyed nothing more than popping the heads off mortals and eating their brains. Not that that bothered Loki.

"Thor's hammer has been stolen," said Loki, swooping down from the sky. "Do you know anything about it?"

"Know about it?" laughed the frost giant coldly. "I took it myself under the cover of darkness, and if the gods ever wish to see it again, they had better send me the beautiful goddess Freyja to be my bride."

Loki returned to Asgard with the bad news. When the lovely Freyja heard the giant's proposition, she was so angry that the walls of the city shook.

"Freyja will not marry a frost giant," said Loki quietly. "If you are to see your hammer again, Thor, we must think of another plan."

The gods met in their great silver hall to decide what to do. Everyone expected the cunning trickster Loki to hatch a plan, but he remained silent. Instead it was Heimdall, the guardian of the rainbow bridge, who had a suggestion.

"There's only one way to get Thor's hammer back. We must dress Thor as a blushing bride," said Heimdall. All the gods apart from Thor burst into laughter. "We must send Thor in disguise, and when the giants reveal where they have put the missing hammer, he can grab it."

Thor was the manliest of all the gods and he didn't like the idea of the others laughing at him dressed as a woman. But he could not think of a better plan, and since all of Asgard was at stake, he agreed.

So that evening a grumpy and embarrassed Thor set off for the giant's homeland, wearing a bride's dress and veil. Loki went with him, disguised as a maidservant.

When they arrived at Thrym's home, the giant was so excited to see his bride that the necklace of human skulls he wore clattered and banged together as he rubbed his snow-grey hands with glee. As was the custom, the happy giant threw a huge feast to welcome his bride. After their travelling, Thor was very hungry and he quickly munched through an entire ox and drank seven horns of delicious mead.

"What an appetite my bride has!" said the giant.

Loki had to think quickly. "Freyja has been so excited

at the thought of marrying you that she hasn't eaten all day," he said from under his disguise.

Thrym leaned closer to his bride, trying to sneak a kiss, and saw that the eyes that lay hidden under the veil burned with anger.

"What furious eyes my bride has," said the giant.

Again Loki had to think quickly. "Freyja is so keen to marry you that she's angry it hasn't happened already," he said.

When the great feast was finally over, the king of the frost giants rubbed his hands together in eager anticipation of his wedding night.

"Let us perform the ceremony so I may marry my beautiful goddess bride who fills me with such joy!" proclaimed Thrym to the assembled mass.

Loki edged his way forward and leant across to whisper in the giant's ear.

"That's very good, my lord, but first there is the small matter of the hammer to be returned..."

"Bring the hammer from its secret hiding place," shouted Thrym.

The king's servants rushed away, and after a moment they returned carrying the hammer. Inside the bride's dress, Thor's heart beat faster and faster as the giants brought Mjollnir closer. He watched each slow step they took until finally, when the hammer was within grasp, he leapt up and grabbed its crimson leather handle.

Thor threw off his disguise and the giants gasped as they saw who had been hiding under the bridal veil all the time. Thrym sprang to his feet to strike a blow at Thor, but the thunder god was too fast and he threw his mighty hammer straight at Thrym's forehead. The hammer smashed clean through the giant's head and burst out the back. Thrym's brains spilled from his broken skull and splattered across the wedding table, colouring it red and grey in equal measure.

At this point, Loki slipped unnoticed from the hall because he had no stomach to see what would happen next. And as it turned out, Loki was the only creature to leave that hall because Thor kept swinging his hammer until every last giant inside was dead.

"And that's the story of how Thor had his hammer stolen, and why no one will ever steal it again," I said, finishing my tale.

Olaf looked at me and actually grinned.

For the last part of the story, while we waited for the silver to melt, Olaf had picked up his own hammer and had been swinging it about, as Thor crushed the giants at the end of the feast. It had obviously put him in a very good mood.

"Thor has killed more giants than anyone in any of the nine worlds," said Olaf, as happy as if he'd slain them himself.

Olaf went to the back of the hut and brought out something hidden in a thick dark cloth. I could see immediately that it was a sword.

"Look at this," he said.

He unwrapped the weapon and held it out to me. It was the most beautiful sword I had ever seen. Olaf made sure I didn't touch it. He held it with the cloth, not even letting his own hands make contact with it. It was double-bladed, both edges were sharp so that in battle the man who wielded it could be twice as deadly.

Olaf turned the sword over and I gasped. On the second side of the sword, the hilt was decorated with a small gold version of Thor's hammer. The pure gold emblem sparkled even in the dim firelight of the workshop.

"It's beautiful," I said, almost lost for words.

"Three days' work left, I reckon," said Olaf. "With a good wind."

Then he refolded the cloth around the sword and put it out of sight. "The silver's ready, we need to pour it," he said.

Olaf had never shown me an unfinished piece of work before. He must have done it because he liked my story, and because of Thor's hammer on the hilt.

"Who's it for?" I said suddenly. I hadn't planned to ask, I just did.

Olaf considered his answer for a moment. He touched his finger gently to his lips, indicating that it was a secret, then he leant forward and very quietly, he said:

"Your father."

My father.

"The time is just right to pour the silver."

My father already had a sword. And he would not order a new sword for himself. It wasn't for him. It couldn't be.

"Careful now. Lift it gently," said Olaf.

I poured the silver. I poured it steadily. I poured it very carefully. I did not spill a single drop. It should have been a moment to remember, but all I could think of was the sword.

"You did it well. Perhaps you have a use in the world after all," said Olaf.

He actually said something that was almost kind. But all I could think of was the sword.

I ran all the way home to our longhouse on the other side of the village. I hadn't set more than two steps inside the house when Mother asked me where the bread pan was. I told her I'd forgotten it – that it was still at Olaf the Smith's and that anyway it didn't matter because we didn't even get around to repairing it, because we made some silver hammers for Thor instead, and I poured the silver and I didn't spill a single drop.

Mother wasn't happy. She started walking around and

asking loudly what was the point of having a son to help you if you sent him to do one simple task and he was away all afternoon. But even though he was away all afternoon, he didn't do that one simple task because he spent all afternoon making amulets for the gods instead?

But I didn't care.

All I could think of was the sword.

The story of the wall

"Stop breaking bits off!" shouted Ragnar, looking down at me and pulling a face.

"I can't help it – it's all loose. You can't put your weight on it!" I shouted back.

We were climbing a rocky cliff overlooking the sea, with the sun hot on our backs. We had different ways of climbing. Ragnar scuttled up the sheer rock face like a spider, his limbs spread out, his body pressed close to the rock. He moved one way, and if he didn't find a safe path upwards, he headed back and tried another direction. I climbed up more carefully. I preferred to check the rocks for hand- and footholds as I went. It was slower, but then I never had to double back.

We called this particular cliff "The Wall". I don't know how high the wall was around Asgard, but I'm sure it wasn't as high as this.

We had left the village on the track that led to the bay where the men were building the new longship. But then, when we reached the cliff, we had turned off the main path and towards the cliff edge. One moment you were standing on solid ground and a few steps later you were on a ledge, the height of twenty men above the sea. Waves crashed on to the sharp brown rocks below us.

You needed a clear day with no rain and not much wind to climb the cliff. If you slipped and fell, you'd die. But we never did.

The ledge ran straight and level, and you could follow it all the way to a narrow point. When you edged around the point and looked up, you saw the nests of a hundred fat, white seabirds scattered over the cliff face above. Each nest was full of eggs.

That morning, Mother had come to find us at the vegetable garden, where she had set us digging, and told us that Magnus had said the birds had finished laying. In past years, one of the men of the village would have been lowered on a rope to collect the eggs. Since we climb the cliff for practice in the summer anyway, it was better to let us collect the eggs. I had a bag with a wide opening hung over my shoulder, so I could put the eggs in using just one hand.

Above me, I saw Ragnar reach his first nest. It was the lowest nest on the cliff and the birds hadn't spotted us yet. Ragnar put a hand into the nest and when he took it out again, he was holding a large white egg. He grinned down at me.

I checked my next handhold, then a foothold, and then I pushed myself up and there was my first nest. It was unguarded. I took two eggs and put them in my bag. The wind was a bit stronger here. It caught the near-empty bag and inflated it like a sail in a storm.

We moved up the cliff, zigzagging from nest to nest. The eggs were large and white, covered with freckles of silver and brown. Some of them were quite beautiful.

If there were six eggs in the nest, I took three. If there were five, I took two. I never left a nest empty. Whenever I could, I collected any loose feathers lying around the nests. They'd be padding for a pillow or quilt when the winter came.

As we worked our way up the cliff, more and more birds became alarmed at our raid and took flight, flapping and squawking, into the air.

"Kee-arr. Kee-arr!"

Their beaks were sharp, and their wings long and powerful. It was best to avoid both. I kept climbing. In some places, the smell of bird droppings was so bad I had to hold my breath.

The sun was still warm, although more clouds were beginning to drift down from the mountains inland. I hadn't told anyone about the sword Olaf showed me. Not Ragnar. Not even Magnus.

Some nests were easier to collect from than others. At one nest, the mother bird wouldn't move and squawked at me, snapping with her beak. I picked up a small piece of rock from the ledge and threw it so that it hit the cliff just behind her, sending the rebounding fragments over her back.

Confused and scared she took off, diving away from the cliff, frantic at leaving her eggs, but relieved to be away from me.

Inside the nest I saw that a piece of falling rock had smashed four of the five eggs. I checked that Ragnar couldn't see me, then I threw out the broken eggs from the nest and replaced them with some from my bag. I moved on quickly.

Climbing The Wall was hard work. Especially edging left and right and up and down to get to each of the nests. I knew the climb would take the whole afternoon and that by the time we got to the top of the cliff and hauled ourselves over, our bags would be full and heavy.

Just over halfway up there was a ledge wide enough to sit on. We planned to meet there for a rest. We'd sit and watch the ocean, and the men in the next bay, building the new longship.

If anyone was looking from the sea, we would have seemed like two strange hunchbacked creatures scaling the cliff like spiders, flanked by an army of grey and white birds riding the winds.

To help me keep going, I thought about the story of the wall around Asgard and the dangerous bet that the gods made to get it built for nothing.

This story happened long ago, when the great wall around Asgard had been destroyed by war and was just a pile of rubble. Shiny black ravens nested between the broken bricks, raising their hungry young in the ruins. The gods of Asgard all knew that the wall needed repairing, but none of them would do the job themselves.

One day, a man on horseback rode along the rainbow bridge that linked Asgard to the world of men. The broad-shouldered man asked Heimdall, guardian of the bridge, for permission to pass so he might speak to the gods, but refused to say why.

Heimdall let him pass and soon the man was standing before Odin and all the gods, except Thor, who was away fighting trolls.

When the man saw that he had the attention of every god in the silver hall, he said, "I am a builder. I'll rebuild your entire wall around the city, and I'll make it higher and sturdier than before so no giant can ever attack Asgard again."

The gods were excited by the prospect of having a new wall, but they knew there'd be a price to pay.

"And all I want for my trouble," continued the builder, "is the sun and the moon from the sky, and Freyja, the fairest of the gods, as my wife. I will need eighteen months from the day I begin."

The builder left the hall of the gods so that they could discuss his idea.

"It's impossible," said Odin. "We can't do without the sun and the moon, and we can't give Freyja away. We'll have to refuse."

But Loki, the trickster god, had an idea. "What if," he said with a cunning smile, "we give the man just six months to build the wall?"

"But no one could do all that work in six months," insisted Heimdall.

The other gods nodded. "No one," they said.

"That's exactly my point," said Loki. "If he won't try, then we lose nothing by asking. And if he takes the condition, then he will fail and we shall have half our wall built for absolutely nothing."

The gods considered Loki's plan and even wise old Odin could find nothing wrong with it.

The builder was called back into the hall and Odin told him that the gods would accept his deal, but that he could only have six months to complete the wall, and that if he did not then he would be paid nothing.

The builder protested, but found that he could not resist the opportunity to win the lovely Freyja's hand, so he finally agreed.

"But I must at least have the help of my horse, Svadifari," the builder said firmly.

"You must work alone," insisted Odin.

It looked like the two sides would never agree, until

Loki leant forward and whispered to Odin, "What does it matter if he uses his horse? He'll never do it."

So, with a sigh, Odin agreed and soon the builder began work.

Each day, the builder would rise before the sun and work all day until well after dark when the moon rose. Often a crowd of gods could be found watching him, and talking about how much of the wall he would get built before the six months were up.

The builder lifted huge boulders that only Thor would have been strong enough to move, and his horse pulled them up the hill in a large net. With the powerful stallion's help, the builder made swift progress, and whether or not he would win the wager became the talk of Asgard.

With only three days left until the end of the six months, Odin stood and frowned at the work. There was now only a small length of the wall left unfinished.

"You got us into this mess, Loki," hissed Odin. "You'd better work out a way to get us out of it, and quickly."

It was now the last night, and the six months were up at dawn. The builder had just one more net-load of stone for his horse to pull up the hill, and he would complete the last section of the wall. He gathered together a pile of massive rocks and put them in the net. But just as he was going to attach the load to his horse, a beautiful mare raced past, flicking her head so her mane glistened in the moonlight. The builder's horse saw the mare and gave chase. The two horses galloped and chased each other all night long, while the angry builder ran after them in desperate pursuit.

By the time the builder had caught his horse, it was nearly dawn, far too late for him to finish the wall in time.

"Agggggggh!"

When he realized he'd failed, the builder let out an angry roar, and to the amazement of the watching crowd, his disguise dropped away. The builder was not a mortal man at all, but a hideous rock giant who had tried to trick the gods. His stony face contorted in hatred and anger at the fact that he had been caught.

"I'll crush you all!" he bellowed, straight at Odin.

He never did though.

Thor had returned from his travels in the east and with a single blow of his hammer he shattered the rock giant's head into a thousand tiny pieces of stone.

The gods gathered up the pieces of the giant's head and body and used them to finish the small section of wall that remained to be built, and so Asgard was safe once more.

No one in Asgard saw Loki for a very long time. Then one day he appeared walking up the rainbow bridge, leading a young horse behind him. The horse had eight legs.

Loki took the animal straight to Odin, who welcomed the trickster. Odin greatly admired the horse, and Loki gave it to him as a gift.

"This horse is named Sleipnir," he said proudly. "He's twice as fast as any four-legged animal. He can race over the seas and the oceans and he can gallop through the sky."

No one ever knew the identity of the horse's mother, although Odin had an idea. And that's the story of how Asgard got its wall, and how Odin took ownership of the eight-legged horse that he still rides today.

On the cliff, seabirds flapped around me as I continued to climb. I reached up and put my hand over the edge of the ledge. Something grabbed it firmly and hauled me up. It was Ragnar. He had got there first, of course.

"Magnus was right. There are lots of eggs," he said. "My bag's nearly full. If I put many more in, they might start breaking against each other."

I crawled across the ledge and sat next to Ragnar with my back against the cliff. I unhitched the bag, now heavy with eggs, and put it on the ledge next to me. Even with the sharp rocks digging into my back, it was a relief to rest.

From this height on the cliff, we could see around to the next little bay where the men were building the new longship. About twenty workers swarmed around the wooden hull.

The men had been working on the ship since the first day of spring. I liked seeing their progress. I wondered whether to go there the next day and help carry wood.

"I wonder if they'll try the same trap again? For the wolf?" said Ragnar.

"Not with Sigund, they won't," I answered.

Ragnar laughed.

A few days before, the men in the village set a trap for One Ear the Wolf. "We've lost too many sheep and goats to do nothing," someone said. So the men drew lots and Sigund the Bloody won – or lost, depending on how you look at it. He had to take one of his goats to the upper pasture, tie it to the ground as bait and then hide in the bushes.

Sigund had never missed a meal in his life, so when he didn't come down for evening food, three men went to look for him. They found the goat gone and Sigund asleep, snoring in the rays of the setting sun. They found the goat on the edge of the forest. It had got loose from the rope and wandered off, which I think made things even worse for Sigund.

"We should kill the wolf," announced Ragnar rather suddenly. He sounded quite serious. "It would be good for when Father comes back. If we kill it, they'd have to take us next time they go raiding."

I nodded. I thought about the sword. I thought about what it would feel like to hold that sword and plunge it into the wolf's side, and…

Something was moving. Out at sea, dark clouds had come into view on the horizon and underneath them something was moving. I could see a black speck getting larger. A long black speck. It was moving towards the shore against the flow of the tide, and this time it wasn't a whale.

"They're coming home!" said Ragnar.

We turned to each other and grinned.

"They're back!"

Father.

A spot of rain hit my face. Then another.

"We might be the first to see them," said Ragnar.

He was probably right. Down on the shore, the men kept hammering and banging on the hull of the new boat. The approaching ship was too far out at sea for them to see it.

I realized that it was suddenly much darker than it should be. Thick grey clouds were rolling out to sea from inland, appearing over the top of the cliff face. More rain hit my face.

"It's going to pour, we need to get off the cliff," I said. "No more eggs, just climb."

There was only one way we could go. Up.

I took a last look out to sea, picked up my bag and started climbing. The wind was stronger now. The birds were all back on their nests, protecting their eggs.

There was a cloudburst overhead and a sheet of rain lashed down. It hit the cliff and ran down the brown rock as a torrent of cold water. It was suddenly very hard to find a handhold and almost impossible to look up to see where I was going.

I heard Ragnar shouting something from above, but when I looked up, the rain stung my eyes. I couldn't hear what he was saying.

I climbed. Handhold to handhold. I passed a bird nestling in a crevice in the rock, safe from the rain.

"Kek-kek-kek!"

The bird looked out at me as if it thought I was mad.

There was a flash of lightning, then a great thunderclap boomed in the distance and rumbled towards me cracking open the sky. Thor was angry and he was shaking the heavens.

I took my next handhold. I couldn't see Ragnar at all now. The wind drove heavy drops of rain at me from every direction.

I wanted to see my father again.

I wanted to hold the sword.

I wanted to kill the wolf.

I spat out rainwater and took my next handhold. As I pushed myself up, my foot slipped and I smacked into the cliff face. I scrambled for something to push against, but I kept slipping. A powerful gust of wind pulled me away from the rock, then just as quickly slammed me back into it. Hard.

I pulled myself up and cut my hand on a sharp edge, but it didn't matter. I had to keep going, handhold to handhold. I had to be near the top now. I had to be.

I looked up and saw a great overhang straight above me – the cliff didn't go up like a sheer wall, it curved out. I knew I could never climb that. I had gone too far to the left. I looked down, but I couldn't go back, there was nothing to hold on to. Rain pelted the cliff.

Suddenly I saw Ragnar through the downpour. He was at the top of the cliff over to the right, where I had been aiming for, but missed. I watched him haul himself over the top and disappear from view.

I waited for him to look over the edge to see where I was. I waited for his face to reappear. It didn't.

I was alone.

I couldn't climb any higher towards the overhang and I couldn't see how to move down. If I let go of the one handhold I had then I would fall.

I would never hold that sword.

I turned my head into the rain and looked out to sea. More than anything I wanted to see my father's ship again, but all I could see was water and grey and clouds and the thrashing summer storm.

Rain beat down hard into my face. I breathed in more rainwater and choked it out. I looked up again, desperate for one more handhold, but the rain just pummelled my face again.

Suddenly I remembered nearly drowning. When I was much younger, years ago, I was swimming in the bay and I went out too deep. A wave crashed into my face and I breathed in and choked. Then I panicked and breathed in more, and with a lungful of seawater I sank down under the water.

"Tor!"

Down there it was completely peaceful. No more struggling to breathe. I remember floating through the water and seeing brightly coloured crabs on the bottom of the sea. And seaweed that was brilliant green.

"Tor!"

"Caw. Caw!"

It was so peaceful, and even though I was very young, I thought, *I suppose I'm going to die*. I remember thinking that while looking at a bright orange crab. And then a great pair of arms grabbed me around the waist and rushed me back through the water to the surface, to the air, and I was choking and gasping again. And it was Ragnar, who was stronger and a better swimmer, who had pulled me out. He saved my life.

Black feathers brushed my face and I opened my eyes. I was still on the cliff face. Still hanging on.

"Caw. Caw!"

Flagg the raven flapped about in front of me, buffeted by the wind.

"Tor! Grab the rope!"

I looked up and there was Ragnar, shouting down from the top of the cliff, dangling a rope in front of my face. I wasn't drowning any more.

I saw Magnus's face look over the cliff top next to Ragnar's. He was straining to see through the rain. Flagg hopped around between us.

Ragnar lowered the rope a bit more. "Be careful, it's slippery!" he yelled.

I took hold of the rope. It didn't matter how slippery it was – I wasn't going to let go.

The story of the storm

My fingers dug deep into the earth and, with help from Ragnar, I pulled myself over the edge of the cliff. I crawled forward on all fours away from the drop and collapsed on wet ground, panting.

There was a sharp purple flash of lightning and then almost immediately afterwards a deep boom of thunder. The gods sounded angry.

"Are you all right?" yelled Ragnar, rolling me over to check.

"I'm fine."

We had to shout to hear each other over the wind and the rain.

Our father's ship was somewhere in this summer storm. The men would need help to land.

"You run to the longboat in the bay and tell the men working there," said Ragnar. "I'll run to the village." But I knew that was the wrong way round.

"You're faster, you go to the bay. They'll need everyone to help," I said, putting down the bag of eggs. A few moments ago they were the most important thing I had, but now they seemed like nothing.

Magnus nodded at Ragnar and we both started running. We were together for a few steps and then we headed in opposite directions.

We had climbed to the top of the cliff so my way back to the village from here was steeply downhill on a winding path that was now mostly mud. I slipped on the first sharp turn and tumbled into the ooze and rushing rainwater. It was probably a good thing, because I didn't care about falling after that. I scrambled downwards, half running, half tumbling, always catching myself and just about keeping control.

I could see the village now. It looked deserted with everyone sheltering indoors. I ran straight to our longhouse and burst through the door.

Mother opened her mouth when she saw me, but she never got the words out.

"The longboat's coming home. We spotted it from the cliff. They'll need help landing!" I shouted.

Without wasting a second, Mother stood up and started telling people what to do. A second later I was gone, running from building to building, shouting into every doorway that I could find.

People began to run down towards the pier. I saw Olaf the Smith come out of a doorway and head in a different direction to everyone else, towards his forge. I wanted to shout for him to come, to help, but I didn't have time.

The wooden pier stuck out into the fjord about the length of two men and it ran along the shore as long as a longboat. I knew Father would head there if he could. In calm weather a longship could land on a flat beach, but not in a storm.

There were lots of people at the pier now. Several of the men had lengths of rope ready to throw out to the men in the longboat so they could try and pull the ship in towards the pier and tie it up.

Someone started asking me how I knew they were coming, when there was a sudden cry from several people in the crowd. I looked up and saw the shape of a dragon's head emerging through the thrashing rain. Next to the wooden figurehead was the ship's lookout. People started waving and shouting, as if the men didn't know where they were going already.

The longship usually had a crew of forty to fifty men. It was the length of over twelve men and the width of three. Perhaps it was because of the way the stormy ocean was rolling the longboat from side to side, but it suddenly looked small and vulnerable. Not like a vessel of war at all.

I focused my eyes on the boat. I saw the ship had several broken oars. The main mast looked as if it was cracked near the base and the sail was nowhere to be seen. They must have had a very rough crossing. I saw two men frantically bailing water over the side using buckets. They were taking on water from the falling rain as well as waves breaking over the sides. The ship listed from right to left as tall waves lashed into it.

One of the men with buckets ducked down again and then I saw what I was looking for. Father.

He was home.

He was acting as the helmsman, looking ahead at the pier, trying to judge the distance and the wind, and he was shouting orders.

Someone said that the steering oar must be damaged because no one on the ship was trying to use it. Several of the men were rowing, but it was a hopeless task. The waves and wind pushed the longboat wherever they liked. First one way and then the other, throwing the bow high in the air and then pulling it down into a trough.

Usually ships drew alongside the wooden pier very gently and were then tied up. I couldn't see that happening today.

The longship surged forward towards the pier. When most of the ship was level with most of the pier, Father gave a signal and the men that still had workable oars tried to slow it down. For a second or two, the ship slowed and looked in control, then the next ocean wave hit from the side and slammed its hull into the pier with a terrible force.

The pier creaked and shuddered. Several women screamed. Another big wave picked the ship up again and crashed it towards the pier. As the ship hit again, some of the crew threw ropes across, but everyone could see it was going to be a hopeless task to try and pull the ship in. Any man that tried it would be yanked off his feet and into the water.

When the next wave pushed the ship near the pier, the men on board began to throw over some of their sea chests. Sea chests are wooden boxes that the men use to store their possessions, and they also double as seats to sit on during the voyage. After a raiding voyage, the boxes being thrown were probably full of gold, silver and other treasures.

As each wave pushed the ship near to or into the pier, it was gradually being emptied of its cargo. Those of us who had stayed on the pier moved the wooden chests and cloth sacks being thrown to us. Whenever the ship hit, we could feel the wooden supports under the pier shift and move.

As its cargo was emptied, the ship got lighter, which meant that it was thrown around by the waves even more.

With most of the cargo now off, one of the crew jumped off the ship when it next lunged towards to the pier. A tangle of arms darted out to grab him and pull him to safety.

When the ship came near again on the next wave, another man jumped, but he leapt too early. He fell into the closing gap between the ship and the pier just as they met. I heard his backbone snap as he was crushed. He disappeared under the waves and a woman at the end of the pier let out a scream and started sobbing.

I saw Olaf get to the edge of the pier. He was carrying a

large bundle of the wooden poles that he had intended to turn into spears. Each was as tall as a man. Olaf threw them down on to the pier, keeping one pole in his hand. Then he stood as near to the edge of the pier as he dared. When the next wave pushed the ship towards the pier, he held out the pole. A man on the ship grabbed it and, as the boat was tossed back, Olaf pulled both pole and man on to the pier.

People rushed for their own poles, to help. The pier creaked whenever the ship battered into it, but finally man after man after man was being pulled from the longship.

I saw one of the men on the ship stagger forward to the bow and pull off the wooden dragon's head and I realized he must think that the ship was going to sink. It made me really sad. I'd never been on an ocean voyage in this ship, but I had travelled up and down the coast and I knew this was a good ship. It knew the tides and stars and the ways of travelling very well.

I think the man who had taken off the dragon's head must have felt the same way, because even in the middle of the terrible storm, with the ship lurching from side to side, he took the time to wrap the figurehead in a cloth sack. And then, instead of throwing it, he chose to jump with it under his arm. He just made it to safety.

One of the new slaves, who had been captured during the raid, was too terrified to jump and had to be practically thrown across.

There were new faces appearing in the crowd around me and I realized that Ragnar had arrived with the men from the next bay.

I grabbed one of Olaf's poles and looked for my father on the ship. If I could line up with him, I could be the one to pull him off. As another wave brought the side of the ship crashing towards the pier once more, I held my pole out to whoever I could help.

I found myself looking straight into the face of a man dressed all in black, with shoulders as wide as an ox. As he saw me ready to try and pull him up, his eyes widened with great surprise as if he knew me. But then he just stared and laughed, and let the wave take the ship out again, without even trying to jump.

The ship was sitting higher in the water now, with just a few men left on board. I was at the front of the crowd and as the next wave thrust the ship towards the pier, I knew that I had to try and pull that man to safety whatever happened. I braced myself and tried to get the best position that I could. I held out my pole and I saw him take the other end. Then, as the wave pulled the ship away, he jumped. He hardly put any weight on the pole at all. His leap was so powerful that he crashed into me and I toppled backwards with him on top.

I think he was the last man off the ship. The longboat was completely empty now and she was very light in the water. Too light.

The waves picked her up, lifted her higher than before, and smashed her into the pier, breaking several of the main supports. The structure creaked and leant forwards, paused for a moment and then slowly fell towards the sea.

It crashed down on to the half-flooded vessel and I saw one of the falling supports break the ship in half. Waves crashed over the broken timber and our old longship disappeared forever.

"You did well," said a voice from behind me.

Father.

The story of treasure

The longhouse was full of smells and smoke, and it seemed like the entire village was squeezed inside, eating and drinking and laughing. It had been three days since the longship came home and of course my father was throwing a feast.

It had taken most of those three days to prepare for it. There were a lot of people to feed. Nearly everyone from our village had returned safely, thank Odin. Only three men hadn't. One had been killed in an ambush during a raid, and another had decided to jump ship and had gone home with a raiding party from Greenland.

Oleg the Beard was the saddest case. Father said that he had fought bravely in battle, worked hard at the oars and was good at navigating by the stars. He had survived the entire voyage and then, when he was a single jump from home, he had slipped; he was the man crushed between the ship and the pier. His wife, Gyda, had hardly stopped crying since. I could see her sitting in the corner of the longhouse. She had come to the feast, but at the same time, she was hardly there at all.

With the old longboat now sunk beneath the waves, many men from further up the coast were stuck here in our village too.

The women had started preparing food almost before the storm that sank the ship had passed. The next morning, men had been sent to the darker forest over the hill to hunt deer. They soon returned with two good adult beasts. On the morning of the feast, Sigund the Bloody toured the pastures and selected (according to him) the best three sheep in the village. No one was surprised that they were all his.

Mother had spent the morning making blood sausages, one of my favourite dishes. As soon as Sigund's three prized sheep were killed, mother slit them open, and took out their intestines, heart, liver and lungs. She cleaned the intestines in a bucket, then chopped all the organs into small pieces and mixed in some garlic. Then she stuffed the mixture into the empty intestines and set them to boil in the second biggest iron cauldron she could find. (The biggest one already had venison stew in it.) The smell of the sheep's insides bubbling away filled the longhouse and made me hungry.

There were more people than there were spaces at the long wooden tables. We were all right though because Ragnar and I were at the top table with Mother and Father. You only had to look at her to see how happy she was that Father was home again. Hanging on the wall behind our table was the spirit of the longboat – the dragon figurehead. It had been cleaned and repainted red and gold for when the new longship was completed.

Slaves hurried around bringing in more food, wild boar

steaks, and then bowls and bowls of the venison stew. You could spot the slaves that had only arrived three days ago very easily.

Across the room, I saw Magnus eating a blood sausage, the tasty juices dripping down his fingers as he pushed it into his mouth. He saw me looking and smiled. Suddenly I realized something was missing. It was odd to see him without Flagg flapping around his feet. Perhaps the raven was enjoying himself outside pecking the last of the flesh off the deer bones.

Sitting next to Magnus was Olaf the Smith. Everyone agreed that his idea to use the spear poles had probably saved many lives. I was watching him closely to see if he talked to Father about the sword.

"Has Father told you any more?" asked Ragnar, leaning close to me.

For a second I thought he was talking about the sword, but of course he wasn't. He meant did I know anything about what had happened on the voyage.

Usually when the longship returned from a raid, the men couldn't wait to tell stories of their adventures and the dangers they'd escaped. This time though they didn't seem to have so many stories to tell.

"No," I said to Ragnar. "Nothing else. I heard Harald the Thread telling the story about the old monk and where he hid the church jewels."

"But that happened on the last voyage!"

"I know. They haven't really said much else. Everyone seems a little quiet."

The treasure haul on this voyage was not as good as usual. There was a set of gold plates and silver bowls (about twenty of each), but that had all come from one unguarded and rather unlucky monastery. (Although it did seem to me to show that our gods, Odin and Thor, were clearly much better and mightier than the Christians' White Christ.)

No one said it clearly, but I was getting the impression that they had found many places that used to be easy to raid to be much better defended this trip, and that they had simply ignored them and searched for easier targets.

"If they let us go with them next time, we can make sure they get more treasure then," said Ragnar.

I decided that attacking places that were so well defended that my father thought a victory unlikely, was probably not the way to begin a long career as a warrior. But Ragnar was right. We were both fast, skilled and quick-witted, and if anyone could make a difference to the next raiding party, it was us.

I had a plan that might help. Ships often changed or even traded crew while away and when our longship returned it had brought Tyral. I thought back to how he had laughed when I tried to pull him from the sinking ship. He was that rarest of all warriors – a berserker.

Berserkers are the most feared fighters on any battlefield. They were more common in war than raiding and I had yet to hear the full story of why he was here. Berserkers wore a shirt made of wild bearskin (called a berserk), and before battle they worked themselves into a killing frenzy that sent them wild as they slaughtered the enemy.

If anyone could teach Ragnar and me more about the skill of raiding and battle it was Tyral. I could see him sitting on the second table with Harald the Thread and his wife, Gudrid. I had never seen anyone look less pleased to have her husband home from a sea voyage than Gudrid did. The pair had sat in stony silence all evening.

Magnus had finished eating and was getting ready to entertain the crowd with his tale of the gods for the evening. While he was talking, I planned to move nearer to Tyral so I could speak to him.

Magnus started his story by pointing to the table where the sets of gold plates and silver bowls were displayed. The crowd cheered when he announced that the story was called "The treasures of the gods".

As dawn broke, Thor's wife, Sif, let out a blood-chilling scream that was heard throughout all of Asgard.

"Aggggggggh!"

Sif was known for her shining golden hair, but this dawn she had woken to find herself completely bald.

Someone had crept into her bedroom under the cover of darkness and cruelly cut off all her hair.

The gods were aghast. Who would do such a terrible thing? Thor thought there was only one person in Asgard who was jealous and mean enough to destroy such beauty.

"Loki!"

Thor was furious and went searching for the culprit. Down in the world of men, the sky filled with thunder and storms just as it did three days ago.

Soon Thor's hand was tightening around Loki's throat, and the mischief-maker was gasping for breath.

"Give me a chance and I'll make amends!" squealed Loki. "I'll go and see the dwarfs. If anyone can make new hair for the Lady Sif, they can."

The other gods persuaded Thor to let go of Loki's neck on the grounds that he could always find it again later, and Loki hurried out of Asgard, muttering under his breath how unfair it all was.

The trickster hurried to the home of the dwarfs hidden deep under the snow-capped mountain we see to the north. Down and down Loki travelled, until eventually he heard the sound of hammers banging on anvils and he knew he had reached his goal.

The three sons of Ivaldi were said to be the most skilled craftsmen of all the dwarfs and they listened as

Loki explained the situation (forgetting to say exactly why Sif needed new hair).

"Only you are skilled enough to do the job," insisted Loki.

"Spare us your flattery, trickster," said the dwarfs. "We'll do what you ask, but not for you, but because the chance to impress Thor and Odin does not come along often in a lifetime."

The three sons of Ivaldi set to work in their dark forge deep under the earth. First they spun gold into threads as fine as a lady's hair. Then the dwarfs spoke strange and powerful words over the threads to give them magic enough to grow on Sif's head. Loki smiled as he watched, knowing that he would again be safe from Thor's wrath.

"We still have a good fire in the forge," said one of the dwarfs. "Let us create something else to impress the gods."

So the dwarfs made a long spear for Odin, the king of the gods, and then a sailing ship as a gift for Freyr, the god of birth and fertility.

Loki was delighted. The gifts would surely win him back favour. As the trickster and shape-changer made his way back through the twisting underground tunnels, his greedy eyes kept glancing down at the gifts and he had an idea.

Instead of going back to the surface, Loki found the hall of the dwarf brothers Brokk and Eitri. Loki knew that these dwarfs were great rivals with the sons of Ivaldi.

"I just wanted to show you their work so you might learn from it," said Loki, as casually as he could. "It's a shame that you two are not skilled enough to make such gifts."

"We can easily outdo those trinkets," said Brokk. "I'll wager my head against yours."

The brothers started work immediately on three more gifts for the gods. As Loki watched them work, he became so impressed with their skill that he began to worry his head might be in danger after all.

Just as the first gift – a boar made of pure gold – was ready to be taken from the fire, a small fly landed on Brokk's hand and bit him. Brokk carried on working and soon the gift was complete. The next gift was a ring of gold and just as it was ready to be pulled from the fire, the fly landed on Brokk's neck and bit him. He ignored the pain and pulled the perfect gold ring from the fire.

The third and final gift was a mighty hammer. Just as it was ready to be taken from the flames, the fly landed right on Brokk's eyelid and bit him so hard that blood ran into his eye. The dwarf cried out and brushed the fly away, and when they pulled the hammer from the fire, they saw that the handle was rather on the short side.

Loki and Brokk now each held three treasures, and it was decided that only the gods themselves could decide which trio of gifts was best and who would lose his head.

Back in Asgard, the council of gods, Odin, Thor and Freyr, listened as Loki boasted how clever he had been and how he had used the dwarfs' rivalry to obtain more gifts. Then it was time for the competition.

Loki stepped forward, confident and sure of himself.

"First, I have golden hair made of real gold for the Lady Sif," said Loki. He put the hair on her head and it magically took root, looking as beautiful as the hair she had lost.

Thor smiled when he saw his wife with golden hair again.

"Next, I have a gift for you, Father, " said Loki. "This great spear is named Gungnir and, once thrown, it will never miss its target. Lastly, for Freyr I have a sailing ship named Skidbladnir. It is large enough to hold all of the gods, but thanks to dwarf magic, it is also small enough to fold up and fit in your pocket."

"It will be hard indeed to beat these gifts," said Odin to the dwarf.

"It is easily done," said the dwarf, sounding more confident than ever. "And if I win, I get to cut off Loki's head."

Loki looked a little embarrassed that now the rest of the gods knew of his bet.

Brokk gave Odin the gold arm ring called Draupnir, and said, "This is a very special ring. Every ninth night, eight new rings of solid gold will drop from it."

Then the dwarf gave Freyr the boar of pure gold and told him that the boar could run faster than anything else in creation.

Brokk's third treasure was a hammer called Mjollnir which he gave to Thor, explaining that it was a very special weapon. "It is so strong that nothing in any of the worlds can break it. And once thrown, it will always return to your hand," said Brokk.

"The handle looks a little short to me," said Loki, with a slight smile.

"That is because a fly bit me on the eye while I was making it. As you know full well," said Brokk, looking straight at Loki, the shape-changer.

The gods decided that the winner was...

"Brokk!" Wise Odin reasoned that, with Thor wielding it, the hammer would keep the gods safe from the giants.

"I have won and I want his head," said Brokk.

Loki had to use all his quick wits to save himself.

"You can claim my head," said Loki, "but according to the bet you may not have any part of my neck."

The gods sadly had to agree with the trickster's logic.

Brokk was furious. "If I may not have your head after all, then at least I will sew your lips together so that you may not speak any more lies!" said Brokk.

The dwarf produced a needle and thread and went to

work, sewing up the mischief-maker's mouth. Loki ran outside with shame and with one quick movement he ripped the thread out of his bleeding lips.

"Aggggggggggh!"

It was the second scream that had echoed through Asgard that day.

People laughed at the thought of Loki running away with blood dripping from his sore lips. Magnus had walked around to our top table. As he finished his story, he stood behind my father and put his hands on my father's shoulders so that everyone would understand that the real treasure that had been brought home was the men of the village.

Everyone cheered and banged their hands on the tables.

I suddenly realized that it was the end of the story and I hadn't moved next to Tyral at all. In fact, I had been so engrossed that I hadn't even noticed that Tyral had got up and left the room. For a great warrior, I could sometimes be very stupid.

I got up and started to search for Tyral. Some of the men were getting very drunk by now and as I passed their table I heard some of them making fun of Sigund the Bloody.

"Next time you go to hunt the wolf, Sigund, remember to take a bed!"

"Call him Sigund the Sleepy!"

Outside it was a perfect summer night and the stars

were bright and clear in the twilight sky. In summer it did not get properly dark. Over to the north, streaks of red and green lights weaved and wandered through the sky. Some people said that the lights were Bifrost, the rainbow bridge to Asgard. Others that they were the souls of warriors killed on the battlefield on their way to Odin in the next life.

I saw Tyral sitting on a stone wall. He was staring up at the sky and holding his drinking horn. He looked sad and like he wanted to be alone. It was the perfect time to ask him if he would be my mentor in combat.

As I walked towards him, he stared at me so hard that I suddenly didn't know what to say.

"You look like my son," he said. "One of them. The eldest."

He was quite drunk. He swayed a little, like a powerful pine tree in a breeze, that might bend, but never fall.

"When the ship was sinking you had the pole. You were going to pull me. But I jumped and saved you getting very wet."

He was a warrior, and warriors are known for their actions and what they do, and not talking that much, so I thought I would get straight to the point.

"I am Tor the Sword, the son of Ivar the Chieftain here in this village. Would you do me and my brother the honour of instructing us in battle and combat?"

He burped very loudly. Then said, "No."

And then he fell over.

I helped him back to his feet and then back on to the wall. He tried draining the cow horn again, but it was long empty.

He looked at me like he was remembering something.

"Three years ago, I was hired by a rich lord to leave my wife and three sons and go to the other end of my country to rid him of a rival lord who wanted to make war. The army of this rival lord was superior in numbers and had better blacksmiths to make better weapons. But we had been on more battlefields and had won more wars. I fasted for nine days and nine nights until in my dreams I was allowed to speak to Tyr, the god of war. I had given him most of my life, my name is taken from his, and he told me what we had to do. It worked. After only four moons, their broken army was scattered over the cold mountains, each man shivering and starving alone. And so I headed home to my family with a sack of gold."

"I want to be a great warrior like you," I said. "I want to be able to tell a story like that."

He suddenly looked utterly lost.

"When I arrived back in my village with my gold, I found that my enemies had already been there. Outside my house were four poles that the men had driven deep into the ground. On top of each of the poles was the head of my wife, and next to her, the heads of my three sons."

I didn't know what to say. For a long moment he looked at me straight in the face, although I don't think it was me that he was seeing.

Then he picked himself up and staggered slowly away into the twilight.

The story of the ship

Everyone was there. Every single man from the village was pushing, or pulling, or moving the tree trunks.

The gods had sent the perfect weather to launch the now finished longboat on to the ocean for the very first time. At dawn, the longboat had still been sitting exactly where it had been built, which was a good ten lengths from the sea. The sun was a ball of fire above us, and it was hot, thirsty work. The longship had to be kept that far away from the ocean in case a summer storm (like the squall that sank the old longboat) or a flood damaged it.

There were around twenty men on each side of the ship, pushing it over the tree trunks towards the sea. As the ship travelled slowly over the tree trunks, the other people (including me) picked up the logs at the back and carried them round to the front of the boat, so it could continue moving. There were around twenty trees under the length of the ship, with another seven or eight being moved from the back of the ship to the front.

It was a slow process and hard work. Very hard work. It was now past midday and the ship had moved about half of its journey to the sea. A few seagulls circled overhead making confused cries as they watched the ship travel over dry land.

"Are you ready this time, Tor?" said Ragnar, as if I wasn't watching and waiting our turn like the entire world of men depended on it.

"Next one."

Ragnar and I were waiting at the back of the ship for the next tree trunk to roll free. You had to be quick or all the men shouted at you. It was vital that nothing stopped the ship moving. We had to get the longboat to the water at exactly high tide when the sea was furthest up the beach. That way it would be lifted clear of any rocks and the tide would help take it out to sea.

"Next!" shouted one of the men as the ship shifted forward. Ragnar and I rushed to one end of the trunk. If you were Tyral you could carry one end by yourself, but if you were Sigund the Bloody then you needed another man to help, like we did.

Ragnar and I put our hands around the end of the tree. It took all our strength to lift it as high as our waist. The other end was suddenly lifted higher into the air and some of the weight disappeared. I looked and saw that Tyral was holding the other end.

"Come on, boys! Odin the Wise has sent us good weather for the launch. Let us not waste it!" he shouted over the noise of the sea and the workers. He held his end of the tree under one arm and started walking.

Tyral had been staying in our longhouse over the weeks since the feast. Occasionally, after he finished working (which he did a lot of) or hunting (which he did even more of) he would help me and Ragnar train for battle.

He had never mentioned his sons again. The only time I heard someone ask him about his family, he just shook his head like he didn't understand. I'm sure I saw him cast a glance at me, but I wasn't going to say anything.

As we carried the tree (which was just as heavy as it looked) down to the front of the ship, the helmsman, who was already on board the longship, started to shout to get the men and slaves to push at the same time.

"Push ... and rest! Push ... and rest!"

He looked very strange, standing on a boat that was sailing across dry land, surrounded by a sea of straining bodies.

"CAW!"

Flagg hopped up on to the ship's bow at the front. Quite a few people stopped work for a moment and looked pleased.

"A raven sitting on the bow brings us good luck!" said Olaf the Smith's assistant, breaking into a cough.

I couldn't see him from the ground, but I knew that Magnus was sitting on board, performing a ceremony asking Odin to grant the ship safe passage during its travels. Sven the Silent was with him and not saying a word, I bet.

We put our tree trunk down at the front of the ship and ran back to the ship's stern.

"Have you heard them arguing again?" Ragnar asked me quietly as we joined the queue of men ready to move the tree trunks. One of the problems of being the son of the village chieftain is that other people often liked to overhear what you were talking about.

"No," I said, leaning close to Ragnar. "Not since then."

Several days after the feast, a boat had brought a message from a chieftain of a much larger village along the coast. The next morning, Mother and Father had a terrible row in their bedroom in the longhouse. I'd only heard them shout like that once before, when Father had brought back a pretty female slave for the house. (He sold the slave the following day.)

We didn't know why they had been arguing. I thought it might be about Father taking us with him on the next raid. Many women did not like it the first time that a father took his sons to fight in case none of them came back.

What we did know was that every hand in the village had been ordered to finish the new longship as quickly as possible. My father and the warrior men, like Tyral, seemed to be waiting for something, but no one had said what.

"Next!"

It was our turn again to pick up a tree trunk. Two thin and scrawny slaves belonging to Asgot the Green got the other end. I probably shouldn't have been, but I was happy to see someone struggling with the weight more than us. The four of us carried it to the front rather slowly.

The new ship had been a long time in the building. It had been started last spring, when Magnus had gone into the forest with the chief carpenters. They had to choose several oak trees and pine trees that were exactly the right length and shape. I went with them, although I had to promise to be quiet and not ask any questions. Magnus told me afterwards that he always tried to choose trees that he thought Odin would be happy to sail in.

After the trees were felled and carried back to the village, they were left to dry out all summer. The following spring, the carpenters set to work. They started by cutting the trunk of the strongest oak tree to be the keel of the boat, which is like its backbone. Curved pieces of wood were joined to it to make the bow at the front (where the dragon head would sit) and the stern at the ship's rear.

Long planks of pine were used to make the hull of the ship. They were attached with thick iron rivets made by Olaf the Smith (some of them were made with my help). The long planks had been carefully riveted on so that each one ran the entire length of the ship. The lower edge of each long plank overlapped the upper edge of the plank beneath it, which meant that the hull could flex a bit and ride the ocean waves instead of fighting them. Magnus told me the ship was "poetry in wood".

Ribs and crossbeams made of wood were added inside the ship. These made the ship strong and would keep it in the right shape. A really heavy block of wood was put right in the centre of the ship. This was really important because it was where the end of the mast would fit, and it needed to be very strong and always keep the mast in place. (A ship with a broken mast at sea was as good as sunk.)

To make the planks along the hull really watertight, the men filled any small gaps with a mixture of animal hair and sticky black tar. Ragnar and I had helped with that for three whole days. The first day we went home with more tar on us than we'd managed to squeeze into the holes.

"It will be a great ship," said Ragnar, for no particular reason, as we watched the slaves push again.

He was right though. And I knew then that we were both hoping it would be the ship that took us on our first raid. Not that we'd had the chance to impress Father much. With most people working to finish the longboat, Old One Ear the wolf had been making easy meals of our animals in the upper pastures. Three sheep had been lost since the last full moon.

One afternoon, Ragnar and I sneaked away from digging at the vegetable plot and went into the forest to look for the wolf. We had a spear, a bow and lots of arrows each. We knew that if we could kill him then no one could question us going on the next raid. We had dreams of sneaking into a forest clearing and killing him as he lay snoring in the summer sun.

We looked all afternoon and then most of the evening, until the twilight made it impossible to tell the trees from the sky. Of course we didn't find the wolf. We didn't even find a footprint.

I saw that Olaf the Smith had appeared in the crowd of women and children watching the ship being launched. He had brought the dragon figurehead. I knew he must have put the finishing touches to that beautiful sword by now and I could almost feel it in my hand, on a raid to take treasure from the monasteries over the sea.

We were making quicker progress now as the longboat had reached the beach where it sloped downhill into the sea. A loud cry went up from the front of the ship as the bow touched the water for the very first time. We picked up another tree trunk and by the time we got it down to the front of the ship we had to splash through salty water before we laid it down.

"Are we supposed to get on board?" Ragnar asked me, shouting over the sound of the breaking waves.

"I don't know," I said. "Let's move one more log and we can see."

Some of the men were now climbing up the side of the ship to get on board as it entered the water. It was a careful balancing act – you wanted as many men as possible on land pushing the ship, but when it entered the water there needed to be enough strong rowers on board to keep it away from the rocks.

I saw Olaf splash through the waves, pass the carefully wrapped figurehead up to anxious hands, and then he was pulled on board himself.

A cheer went up from the crowd as the ship slid forward. I felt a great pride in what the village had done.

"Ragnar! Tor!"

I saw my father appear at the stern of the ship. He gestured to us to get on board. The whole of the ship was in the water now, and we went splashing through the waves to catch up.

Someone threw a rope down and Ragnar caught it. He half jumped and half pulled himself up on it, and a flurry of thick-fingered hands grabbed and hauled him the rest of the way.

The rope reappeared, I grabbed it, lost my footing on a boulder, and fell forward, crashing into the hard, wooden stern post. As I fell back towards the water, I felt a hand grab the back of my shirt. It threw me up towards the side of the ship, and I just about managed to grab hold before more hands heaved me on board. A few moments later, Tyral, refusing all help, climbed over the side of the ship.

Ragnar pulled me to my feet. We were both soaking wet, but the sun would soon dry us.

The deck of the ship was a very busy place. Men were

passing oars to each other and putting them through the ten small holes that ran along both sides of the ship. Olaf was fixing the dragon head in position, helped by Magnus.

I saw Father walking towards us with the helmsman following him. He stopped and looked at Ragnar and me for a moment without saying anything. I don't know what he was thinking, but he looked really proud, although I don't know why.

"Helmsman, teach them to row," he said simply.

Yes.

That meant we were going to be part of the crew. That meant we were going on a proper voyage. And that meant we were going raiding.

Ragnar and I smiled at each other. Really big smiles. We didn't need to say anything.

The men sat on their sea chests, two men for every oar. I sat next to Ragnar and took hold of the oar with both my hands. Of course we had both rowed small boats many times before, but being part of a crew, taking shifts and rowing across the open ocean was different.

Just as we were about to start, someone tapped Ragnar on the shoulder. "You're in my seat," said Tyral, although Ragnar wasn't of course. But I supposed Tyral could sit anywhere he liked.

At first I was a bit sorry that I wouldn't be rowing with Ragnar. When we got moving though, I quickly realized

I needed someone like Tyral to help keep me in time with the other rowers. Not to mention someone strong to help do the actual rowing.

We rowed the longboat towards the end of the inlet and the open sea. It was perfect. The sun was hot and the sky was blue and clear, and now that we were away from the shore, there was a good cooling breeze as we worked, pulling hard on the oar to make it cut through the water. Ragnar was two oars in front of me and I saw him turn round and smile. It really was perfect.

As we left our inlet for the open water, we could feel the waves and wind and tides change. They were suddenly more powerful and less forgiving.

We were at sea.

The helmsman gave the order to stop rowing. From some secret place under the deck, he brought out two small barrels full of Father's home-brewed beer. There was only enough for a mouthful each as they were passed man to man to man, but it was the best thing I had ever tasted.

While the helmsman and my father watched and listened as they let the ship ride the waves, I looked back to shore. I loved the view from out at sea.

I could see our village, hardly any smoke rising from the houses today as everyone was crowded down at the beach. The figures were small now and I couldn't tell who was who any more. I could see the pastures rising steeply towards the dark green forest, and beyond that the mountains with their peaks brilliant white in the sun. This must be what it was like to look down at the world if you were one of the gods sitting in Asgard.

One of the men passed the beer barrel back to me. I took it with both hands and he slapped me on the back. I was happy. I was sure that my father had commissioned that wonderful sword for me as a surprise for my first raid. I had a place on the crew of a fast and strong longship. And I had my best friend and brother, Ragnar, at my side.

I had absolutely no idea how things were about to go horribly wrong.

There were gasps from some of the men behind me and I turned to see what they were looking at. The men were starring along the coast. Past the cliff with the birds' nests. Past the next cliff, and the next and the next. They were looking to where the coast curved north and you couldn't see land any more.

A huge longboat was moving into view. Its red and white striped sail was puffed out by the wind. Behind it was another longship, then another and another. I counted fifteen, twenty, twenty-five, then I lost count as they moved across each other and through the heat haze on the horizon.

Tyral looked at the ships hard, but there was no emotion on his face.

"War is coming," he said.

The story of the sword

A lot happened very quickly after that. We rowed our ship back to the village and stood on the beach with everyone else to wait for the fleet of ships to appear at the entrance to our inlet. I've never seen people look so worried. You'd have thought that Ragnarok – the Doom of the Gods – was upon us.

"Are they going to attack?" I asked Magnus as the first ship appeared, and a gasp went up from the crowd.

"No," he said. "People are more worried about their food and their wives."

Ship after ship after ship appeared, but they all kept sailing past the entrance to our inlet without turning into it.

"If they stopped to stay overnight in our village, then we would have to provide them with food and drink," explained Magnus. "If there are as many ships as you say, there could be ... two thousand men on board. I know villages that have been ruined by such a fleet stopping for a single night. Eaten out of house and home."

I tried to imagine what two thousand men would look like, but I couldn't really manage it. Our village (even including the extra men who hadn't returned home yet) had perhaps three hundred men, women and children.

Ragnar and I left the others at the beach and ran up to the cliff top where we could look out. Some of children followed us, chasing behind, but this wasn't a game.

We knew what was happening now. Father had told everyone on the beach. The last raiding expedition had returned with less treasure than usual because they'd found the coast much better defended than they'd expected. Other raiding ships had found the same thing and now a combined fleet of ships was going to sail together to break the defences. We were to sail soon and catch up with them.

We watched the ships go past and counted thirty-two. Many had white and red sails; many had their sails dyed blood red. On most of the ships multicoloured battle shields were displayed on a shield rack that ran along the side of the ship. The decks were crowded with men ready to fight.

The children were excited at seeing so many ships and started to play at being invaders. For Ragnar and me though it was different.

"This isn't going to be just a raid. This will be war," I said to Ragnar, echoing Tyral's words.

He just nodded and we watched the fleet of ships disappearing south.

Over the next few days, a different mood settled over the village. People had been cheering as we launched the ship, but now they became quiet and apprehensive. Many of the women did not want their husbands to sail to a war, but our village was expected to provide a longboat of men to join the fleet or we would be considered cowards and completely dishonoured.

Father instructed us in battle training himself, for the first time in ages. (He was usually too busy.) And when he couldn't do it, he had Tyral do it instead. We practised combat with sword and spear, and archery with a bow and arrows. One afternoon I saw Mother watching Ragnar and me, but instead of looking proud or pleased as she usually did, her face was drawn. For the first time I could see fear in her eyes.

Magnus made it exactly clear what Mother was afraid of. Walking past the graveyard one evening, he took me inside and reminded me how many of the people buried there were women and children, and how few of the people were grown men. Most of the men had been lost at sea or on the battlefield. Only a few had died at home. And even fewer had died of old age. It made me think.

For three days running we sailed the new ship out to sea, raised the mast and the new sails that the women had made. We tested our ship against wind and waves. The ceremony to name the longboat was performed by Magnus in front of all the men who were going to sail. Our new ship was called the *Flying Serpent* in the hope of a fast voyage and a swift return home.

After that, everyone began loading up the ship in earnest, ready for the voyage. Each man had his own sea chest that he would sit on while rowing, which doubled as his personal store. Most of the chests stored weapons, but others took things like walrus tusks or amber beads in the hope of trading them for a profit somewhere along the voyage.

Harald the Thread sat outside his house and worked for three days and three nights without sleep, making a banner for the battlefield. The banner had a black raven with its wings spread against a white background.

"There were once three sisters," he told me, and anyone who would stop and listen, "who wove a banner between one midday and the next, having worked all night. The banner had magical properties for its chief on the battlefield and provided an omen of what was yet to be. If it was carried forward on the battlefield and a living raven appeared on the banner, then the chief would win a great victory. If the raven on the banner hung still and stark, then the battle was going to go badly."

We nodded and told him that we were sure that Father would be grateful. Harald loved that kind of thing, but if you were already on the battlefield surrounded by enemy warriors trying to kill you and all your friends, then you might think it was a bit late for the news of your imminent defeat to be of any use, I thought. But I didn't say that.

The afternoon before we sailed, Ragnar and I spent time

training with each other. We used two of the heaviest swords we could find and practised moving and blocking and hitting with them.

"We should swing them as hard as we can," I said. "Just to get used to taking the blows on our swords instead of our shields. In case we have to in battle."

"You ready then?" said Ragnar, preparing to strike a blow at full strength, holding his sword in two hands.

"I'm ready."

He drew his sword back and brought it smashing down on mine. The metal shuddered in my hand. I made sure he was ready then hit Ragnar's sword as hard as I could. I knew that when I had my new sword, I would best him easily.

"We should do a fight. Like for real, but slower," I suggested.

We circled round each other, taking it in turn to land blows on the swords. The swings got faster and closer together. Sword swing then block. Sword swing then block. I raised my sword again and Ragnar, waiting until the last moment, suddenly moved his weapon out of the way. From then on that became part of how we did it.

We went faster and faster. Swing then block. Swing then miss. Swing then ... Ragnar should have blocked me, but instead he moved quickly to the side and kicked the back of my knee so I fell to the ground. He put his foot across the flat of my sword pinning it to the ground.

"Ha – got you!" he said, pointing the tip of his own sword under my chin like he'd won or something.

"That was really unfair!" I said.

"There's no need to shout."

"I'm not shouting!" I said quietly.

"You are."

"But that really hurt and it wasn't what we were playing," I said, picking up my sword from the dirt. Then I saw Father heading towards us. I hoped he hadn't seen me on the ground.

"I've got enough to do without you two fighting," he said gruffly. He looked really serious. "Ragnar, get back to the longhouse. You need to have your chain mail checked. Tor, I need you to run over to Olaf's. He'll give you a package. Bring it straight back to the longhouse. Understand?"

"Yes, Father," we said almost at the same time.

I ran all the way to Olaf's. I was still angry at Ragnar. He was a summer older than me, and it was bad enough that he was stronger and taller without Father seeing him knock me off my feet, even if we were just playing.

"Did you never learn to knock?" said Olaf as I walked in.

"Father says you have something for him. He sent me to get it," I said.

Father was taking a few metal-working tools away on the ship in case any weapons needed repairing during our voyage.

"Are you feeling all right?" said Olaf, which was a stupid question.

"Of course I'm all right," I said. It was really hot in his forge, and smoky too.

"I thought you wanted to sail with the raiding men," he said.

"I do," I said. "Look, do you have the package for my father or not?"

He walked round the charcoal fire to where the battle shields always hung on the wall. When he came back, he thrust an object wrapped up in cloth at my chest.

"There. Now go," he said. "You know what it is."

It was the sword. The sword.

I didn't say anything else, I just stepped outside. I was holding the sword. I started walking back to the longhouse so that Father could give the sword to me.

But then I stopped. Why would he send me to get the sword if it was for me? He'd want it to be a surprise, wouldn't he? I realized then it wasn't for me. It was for Ragnar. He was older than me. He was getting his own sword before I did. It was for him. How could he give Ragnar a sword and not me?

As I walked home, I heard a voice greet me. "Hello, Tor." I didn't know who it was because I didn't look. When I got to the door of the longhouse, Father opened it like he'd been waiting for me.

"I thought I told you to run," he said, taking the package. "Carry on with your training." He shut the door, making it clear that I should stay outside.

I turned around and saw Ragnar walking slowly towards me.

"I had to get new chain mail," he said patting his chest. I saw he was wearing a shirt of chain mail. "I grew too much for the last one."

The sword was definitely for him.

"Are you all right?" he asked. "What's the matter? I'm sorry about before."

"I'm fine," I said, pushing him in the chest. "Stop asking me if I'm all right."

"What are you doing?"

"Nothing," I said, pushing him again.

"Get off!"

I swung a punch at Ragnar and hit him on the shoulder. The chain mail hurt my hand. I was really angry now.

"The sword's for you!" I said.

"What sword?"

I tried to punch him again, but he sidestepped my swing and got me in a headlock, twisting my neck to try and keep me still. It hurt.

"Calm down."

"Get off me! You're not even his real son!" I said.

As soon as I said that, even then, I wished I hadn't. Ragnar looked really shocked. He was already off balance and the weight of the chain mail sent him crashing to the muddy ground. I jumped on top of him and punched him in the face. Twice. The first time I heard his jaw snap shut. The second time I think I hit a tooth.

A hand grabbed the back of my shirt and lifted me straight up into the air. My legs swung, searching for the ground.

"Tor! What in Odin's name are you doing?" Father shouted straight in my face. He rarely shouted at anybody, because he never needed to.

I saw our fight had already drawn a small crowd.

"Inside!"

Father pushed me through the door of the longhouse. Before he shut the door behind him, I saw three things I would never forget.

I saw Mother leaning over Ragnar wiping blood from his mouth. I saw the look in Ragnar's eyes as he stared at me. And I saw Tyral standing by the door of the longhouse. He must have been inside with Father the whole time.

I looked at Tyral. I saw the confusion on his face. And I saw the new sword that was hanging from his belt.

I just had time to see that the hilt was decorated with a small gold image of Thor's hammer before the door slammed shut.

The story of the god who was afraid

We set sail the next morning. The start of the voyage had come quicker than I wanted. The sky was full of thick grey clouds that looked dirty, like snow under soldiers' boots. They seemed so dense that I wondered if the gods in Asgard could still see down to earth. I didn't like the idea of them not being able to see what was happening to me.

I felt terrible about the fight with Ragnar and what I had said to him. Father was furious. Of course I had said sorry to Ragnar, but he hadn't spoken to me since, and I didn't know if he hated me or not. He probably did, and it made me feel sick in my stomach to think that. In a way, worrying about Ragnar and about what a stupid idiot I'd been, took my mind off leaving Mother and the fact that we were probably all going to be slaughtered and have our heads put on poles in front of someone's house.

As we rowed away from the rebuilt pier, leaving our village behind, I could see that a lot of the women were crying. This was the first time that Mother had been left alone since I was born. I could see Magnus standing next to her, waving.

"Your friend is here," said Tyral, sitting next to me and pulling with me on our oar. His new sword was payment for his services as a mercenary and I was glad it was hidden away in his sea chest where I didn't have to look at it. The friend he was talking about was Flagg, who had zigzagged across the water and landed on the side of the ship next to me. A contented murmur went around the men who saw the bird land. Ravens were good luck. At that moment, it felt as if Flagg was the only friend I had in all Midgard.

We pulled a stroke on the oar and Flagg took off, flying back to Magnus. He repeated the journey as our longship drew further and further away from land. The third time Flagg landed, he stayed longer and I knew that this time when he flew away he would not return. I wanted to go with him. If I could have changed shape like Odin, or even Loki, then I would have changed into a raven and flown back to Mother with Flagg leading the way home. I didn't want to go to war. And I especially didn't want to go to war in a ship with a father and a brother who hated me.

We had passed through the mouth of our inlet now and were at sea. As we turned to head south, the village disappeared from view and I felt homesick already.

We kept rowing until midday, when the sun was highest in the sky, but we didn't stop then. We kept rowing until we passed the great grey cliffs to the south and then we carefully raised the mast, ready for the sails. Raising the mast is one of the most dangerous things to do at sea, because it is very heavy and if handled wrongly it could easily unbalance the ship. With our sails up, we caught a good strong southerly wind and headed on down the coast.

I looked over the side. Now the ship was loaded with a full crew, the ocean's surface was only about an arm's length away. That didn't seem very much compared to the size of some of the waves. I noticed that the ship felt most balanced and safe when we were moving forward. When we were drifting (like when we had stopped to drink the barrels of beer on launch day), the ship was tossed and turned by the waves instead of travelling over them. As we cut a speedy path down the coast, riding on the winds, the ship did start to feel like "poetry in wood".

Our plan was to follow the coast south as far as we could and then cut across open ocean using the shortest route, so that we were out of sight of land for the least amount of time possible. When he can't see land, the helmsman will navigate using the position of the sun in the day and the stars at night. He'll watch carefully for seabirds flying home or cloud formations on the horizon – anything that might tell him where there is land.

If the wind died down, then we would use the oars again. From then on though only half the crew would row at any one time, while the other half rested. That way, if we needed to, the ship could keep going for hours and hours.

I knew from listening to many tales told during feasts that a sailor's great fears were large waves that could roll the ship over and, most of all, sinking out of sight of land. I tried not to watch the waves breaking against the ship's hull, but sometimes it was difficult not to, just to make sure they weren't too high.

"Do you know the rooms?" Tyral asked me.

I said I did and I told him what they were.

The ship is divided up into six sections or "rooms". Each room is like a family of men that work together, talk together and eat together. The six rooms have different jobs.

At the bow (front) of the ship is the foreship, which includes the lookout. Then there's the tack, then the midship, which includes the mast and all the ropes that go with it. The next room is the drag room; part of that room's job is to make sure the sails never catch on anything. Next comes the aft and then, at the stern (back) of the ship, is the lifting where my father, the helmsman, and the first mate all stood, so they could see everything that was happening on the ship in front of them. The lifting also had the steering oar.

When rowing, the men sat so that they were looking behind the boat. I was in the foreship and Ragnar was in front of me, in the tack.

No cooking was allowed on board in case it set fire to the wooden boat, which would be a disaster. When we were close to the coast, the cook would go ashore three times a day. He went twice to cook a hot meal for everyone and once to get fresh water.

With the sails up and the wind in the right direction, there was not much to do apart from sit and watch the cliffs go by and the sun sink towards the horizon in the west.

"The deck is too new!" announced Tyral, getting out his knife and beginning to carve a hneftafl board into the wood. Hneftafl is a board game where one player has to protect his king from the attacks of the other.

I asked Tyral why it was that we went on raiding expeditions to other lands, but that no one sailed across the sea to attack us in our homes.

"It might be because we're always short of good land here to grow crops or tend animals. You cannot farm or keep animals on your higher pastures in the winter. You'd die. I'll wager it is hard enough staying alive in your longhouse through the worst of the cold," he said.

Then he thought some more and said that it might be because we have the best ships.

"Our longboats travel swiftly," he explained proudly. "They hold many good men and can manoeuvre under sail if there is wind, or by the crew rowing if there is none. The hull does not sit deeply in the water, so although the boats are strong enough to cross the open ocean, a longship can also sail up a shallow river or land on a beach and surprise the enemy."

If our ships were so much better than everyone else's, I wondered, then why didn't they just copy the design and then sail across the sea and raid our villages? Tyral stopped carving his game board and looked up at me, and I knew that it was time to stop asking things because I didn't want to be called Tor the Question again.

My hands were blistered and sore from rowing for so long. Most of the men were used to it, but Ragnar and I weren't, and I guessed his hands would be just as sore as mine.

I wanted to go and say something to Ragnar, but I didn't know what. So after the evening meal, I just got into my sleeping bag and curled up on the deck with the other men. Although it had been a warm day, it was a lot colder now, with a clear sky and the wind from the open ocean. I tried to go to sleep, but the boat was rocking and I could hear the waves hitting the side of the hull. I felt really miserable.

I opened my eyes to look at the stars and I saw that Tyral was looking down at me. I wasn't crying or anything, but I think he knew that I wasn't very happy.

He pressed his finger to his lips, telling me to be quiet, then he moved nearer and started telling me the story of Loki's three monstrous children.

In Asgard, it was a night darker than any other had ever been. The gods lay awake in their beds so full of fear and nightmares that they could not sleep. The cause of their nightmares was Loki's three hideous children, for it had been foretold that they would bring great doom to the gods.

After nightfall, Loki had often sneaked out of Asgard and ridden to Jotunheim, the land of the giants. There he'd had great pleasure in the arms of the giantess Angrboda, who had over the years born him three monstrous offspring.

The oldest child was Fenris, a ferocious wolf with powerful jaws and huge teeth. The middle child was Jormungard, who was already the longest serpent in all creation with thick and deadly coils. The youngest child was called Hel, a pale-skinned girl whose body was half alive and half dead. Any room she entered soon stank with the stench of the flesh rotting on her bones.

Odin decided, and all the gods agreed, that something had to be done. The next night, the gods travelled to Jotunheim under the cover of darkness and kidnapped Loki's children, bringing them back to Asgard.

When it was done, Odin looked at Loki's three offspring in horror, but at the same time he knew that he could not kill them and stain Asgard with their blood.

Odin saw that Hel's body was half alive and half dead, so he cast her out of Asgard and into Niflheim, the underworld realm of the dead.

"You will be the Queen of the Dead and you will

receive the souls of all those who do not die in battle but die because they are ill or old," he told her.

Then Odin turned to the slithering mass of coils that was Jormungard. With one mighty throw, Odin sent him tumbling out of Asgard and all the way to Midgard where he landed with a terrible splash in the ocean. Jormungard stayed hidden at the bottom of the dark ocean, feeding and growing every day, for many years. In time, he grew so long that he encircled the whole earth and lay there with his own tail in his mouth. He became the Midgard Serpent and he lies under this ship as we sit here tonight.

Odin decided that Fenris the wolf should remain in Asgard where the gods themselves could watch over him. Tyr, one of Odin's sons, was the only person brave enough to go near Fenris to feed him, and every day he would throw chunks of raw meat dripping with blood into the wolf's hungry jaws. Fenris grew bigger and bigger, and demanded more and more meat.

The gods saw how Fenris was becoming larger and became more worried than ever. When a prediction was made that one day Fenris would devour All-Father Odin himself, everyone agreed that something had to be done about the wolf. The gods devised a plan to trick Fenris into letting them bind him with a chain of strong iron that he would never break.

The gods showed Fenris the chain and said, "This is a

chain made by gods. A simple wolf like you could never break a powerful chain like this."

Fenris looked at the chain with disgust. "It's a strong chain to be sure, but it's not as strong as me," he said.

He allowed the gods, who were nervous about being so close to his jaws, to wind the chain around his neck and body and all his limbs until he could not move. When he was bound, the gods were greatly relieved and secretly smiled to each other. Fenris took a deep breath and tightened his muscles, and a moment later he burst free from the chain.

"I'm hungry," snarled Fenris. "Feed me."

The gods quickly made another chain twice as strong as the first. Again they approached Fenris and said, "This is a much stronger chain. If any creature could break this chain, then stories of his great strength would be told forever throughout all the worlds."

Fenris looked at the chain and saw that it looked stronger than the last.

"No one wins fame without taking a chance," said Fenris, once more letting the gods tie him tightly. When they had finished binding him, Fenris took a breath, tightened his muscles again and strained to be free. He could not break the chain, and the gods were greatly relieved and secretly smiled to each other.

Fenris threw himself to the ground and struggled and

rolled and strained. Then he rose to his feet, licked his wolf lips and burst the chain, sending so many pieces of broken iron flying through the air that even the gods had to duck.

Now the gods were very worried, but Odin suggested the answer. "We will ask the dwarfs for a magical enchanted chain to bind Fenris," he said. "Send the request with a payment of gold."

A short time later, a messenger brought the chain to Odin. It was called Gleipnir and it was as slight and as light as a thin silk ribbon. Even Odin wondered if the dwarfs were playing a trick.

The gods invited Fenris to accompany them on a hunting trip. As they all rested in the afternoon, Odin took the ribbon from his pocket and once more challenged Fenris to break free of the new chain.

"That chain is so puny, where would be the honour in breaking it?" said Fenris, ripping out pieces of flesh from a deer they had caught.

"It's stronger than it looks," said Odin.

"If there is magic in it, then I'll probably never get it off. And I don't trust you to release me if I can't. But on the other hand, I don't want anyone thinking I'm a coward. I'll let you bind me with your little ribbon as long as one of you puts your hand in my mouth," said Fenris, with a smile that showed all his teeth.

The gods couldn't look each other in the eye. No one wanted to put his hand in the mouth of the wolf for he would lose it for certain. There was a very long and very awkward silence until Tyr said, "All right, Fenris, I'll do it." Tyr was just as afraid of the wolf's jaws as the other gods, but he was the bravest of them all because he did it anyway.

So Tyr put his hand into the wolf's mouth and Fenris was bound by the magical chain, and of course could not break free. The more he struggled, the tighter the chain became. The gods were very relieved and smiled openly to each other until they heard a terrible snarling and then a scream.

When the gods looked, they saw that Tyr now had a bloody and bleeding stump where his hand used to be.

The gods took Fenris deep underground and secured his chain to a huge rock. As he tried to bite them, Thor jammed his sword into the wolf's mouth, propping it open. Then they left Fenris alone in the blackness, with only his own terrible howls for company.

Loki's children are still there today. Hel waits in the gloomy realm of the dead collecting souls. The Midgard Serpent lies coiled at the bottom of the ocean under this very ship. And poor Fenris waits chained in his deep, dark, underground prison. They all wait for the Day of Ragnarok, the Doom of the Gods, when they can take their hateful and terrible revenge.

I had heard the story many times before of course. This time I found it strangely comforting to think that the same giant serpent at the bottom of the ocean under our ship, would also stretch as far as the ocean near our village.

I fell asleep and dreamt of monsters.

The story of the boy who was brave

The rocks were so slippery I wished I'd taken a spear like Father had said. I'd decided it would be easier to crawl over the rocks on all fours, but I was wrong. I had got so near to the seal that I needed to stand up. It wasn't easy. The rocks were covered with light-green seaweed that made your feet slip as if they were greased with whale fat.

As I got to my feet, I nearly slipped straight over and a loud cheer went up from the longboat. As the youngest member of the crew, they said it was tradition that I should make the first proper kill of the voyage. (Fish on a line didn't count.) I wasn't so sure if it really was a tradition or if they just wanted to see me get wet.

Ragnar had edged across the slippery rocks towards me.

"I'll help you pull it back to the ship," he said. It was the first time he'd spoken to me since the fight.

"I'm really sorry," I said.

We were standing on a rocky outcrop in the middle of the ocean with the tide lapping at our feet, with the longship drifting dangerously close to the rocks. But the only thing that mattered to me was for Ragnar to know how sorry I was.

I saw him think for a moment, then he said, "I thought we were blood brothers."

"We are. I didn't mean what I said. I was being stupid."

"Kill it!" someone shouted from the ship.

"In Odin's name, get on with it!" yelled someone else.

Ragnar and I couldn't help but smile – as usual the adults were chasing us about jobs.

I raised my sword high over my right shoulder, ready to strike. Then I looked down straight into the seal's eyes, and saw they were as black as an empty cauldron.

I could feel my hands tremble a little. I'd never killed a seal before. And I'd never killed anything with so many people watching. The seal just looked up blankly. For a moment, I didn't know if I was going to swing my blade down or not, but then I brought it down as hard as I could, slicing through the seal's neck and killing it with a single blow.

Another cheer went up from the longboat. The men had been on the open ocean for two days and two nights and any amusement was very welcome.

Between us we dragged the seal to the boat and it was lifted on board by stronger arms than ours. Then we rowed away from the small rocky island, heading south along the coast of the Shetlands, looking for somewhere to land to cook the seal for our evening meal.

The gods had been kind and had given us a good ocean crossing over the last few days. Only the second night had been a trial. The sea had been choppy enough to make it difficult to sleep, and then in the middle of the night it started to pour with rain.

We had to use buckets to empty the rainwater out of the ship. Someone had to go down into the dark space between the deck and the hull. That someone had to be small, so again they picked me. There was never any great danger that the *Flying Serpent* would fill with rainwater, but in the middle of the night, bailing out water was cold, wet and miserable work. After passing up the first few buckets, Ragnar joined me in the dark, cramped space under the deck. We didn't say a word to each other as we worked, and at the time I hoped it meant he didn't hate me.

Dawn couldn't come quickly enough for me that particular night. When the sun finally appeared, the entire ship, the timbers, the sails and even the men began to steam as the sun burned off the water.

For the next day, we continued sailing south, passing along the east coast of the Earldom of Orkney (more small, flat islands) heading to our destination – the Kingdom of the Scots.

The last few raiding missions that had come to this section of coast had found it much better defended than they'd expected. We were part of a loose fleet sailing together to break those defences so that our profitable raids on settlements and monasteries on rivers and the coast could continue.

"In the south of the country, the Danes don't even need to go raiding to get their money," Harald the Thread explained to us with great relish as we rowed. "The English are so cowardly that when Danish raiders arrive, rather than fight them, they buy them off by giving them protection money as gafol."

"Gafol" means tribute. I'd also heard the money called "Danegeld" which means Dane-gold.

"They hope the silver they give away as gafol will prevent the raiders from coming back, but of course they always do. Or different raiders do. Either way, the English end up paying again. Svein Forkbeard, the King of Denmark, has got rich and fat on his Danegeld and I don't blame him. It's easy money. I'd enjoy taking a sack of silver in exchange for doing nothing," laughed Harald.

I heard Tyral grunt with disapproval.

"Mortal men are not put on earth to enjoy themselves," said Tyral loudly as we pulled back on the oar. "We are here to honour the gods."

He sounded like he really meant it too, and after that everyone was very quiet.

The men stayed quiet as we travelled on along the coast. Craggy brown cliffs led up to dark green forests of pine. We all knew that we would soon be pulling the longship ashore and then we would be fighting. Ragnar often looked back and smiled at me and I felt I had undone much of the damage.

For the first time I felt I understood something I had seen before but had never been part of – the closeness of a group of men after a long voyage. I had seen it many times when the old longship had returned. Now I felt part of it too.

The helmsman shouted an order and one side of the ship stopped rowing, and we turned in towards a shallow inlet. This was a route they obviously knew well. I felt the keel scraping against the shingle and watched men jump over the bow to wade ashore and guide in the ship.

The first sight that greeted us was not good. Being tossed backwards and forwards by the breaking waves was a battle banner – a black wolf on a white background. It was tatty and torn and drenched in blood as if it had been used to soak up some great wound. A spear lay alongside the banner, broken into two pieces.

Most of the men saw it, but no one said anything. We made our preparations and moved on as quickly as we could.

A few of the men were chosen to stay and guard the longship. For a moment, I didn't know if I wanted to be one of those men or not. It seemed a better way of spending time than marching to a battlefield, but I did not want to be separated from my father and brother and Tyral. I wasn't chosen anyway, and the moment passed.

If there was a time and place set for the attack, I didn't know what it was, but for once I didn't feel like asking questions.

We headed steeply uphill and inland. With the men walking next to each other, you could see how much their fighting equipment varied from man to man. Men without much money had only a leather cap to protect their head and a padded leather tunic over their chest.

Men like my father, and professional soldiers like Tyral, wore iron helmets and long chain-mail tunics that went down to below their waist. A good chain-mail tunic could stop anything except a really well-aimed blow from a sword.

Their weapons varied too, from spears and simple iron swords, like I'd seen Olaf the Smith make a dozen times, to weapons beautifully encrusted with silver and gold, like my father's and Tyral's swords. A good sword is a warrior's most prized possession, and if he follows the old ways and the old gods then his sword will probably be buried with him. Tyral now carried two swords on his belt – the sword that father had given him, and his own highly prized blade that he called "Dragon's Fang".

We had been walking most of the morning and the helmsman (still leading the party even though we were on dry land) signalled that we were going to take a break. I went into the forest away from the others to take a pee. The forest smelled different from home. As I stood there, I heard a noise like a whimpering dog coming from the clearing beyond some thick pine trees. I edged into the clearing, sword ready in my hand in case it was an animal we could eat.

Lying on the ground was a warrior in a terrible state. A section of his right shoulder had been half hacked away by a sword blow and hung down from his body. He was pressing his hands against his stomach, where there was a deep gash. He looked like he was trying to hold the wound together, without much success. There was a trail of blood and mess in the undergrowth where he must have been dragging himself along.

Our eyes met. We were both surprised to see each other. He tried to say something, but instead of words, his mouth produced a mixture of blood and froth that dribbled pitifully down his chin.

He tried again.

"Kill me … please."

He must have been in awful pain.

I drew my sword and approached him.

I had never killed a man before.

When he saw the blade of my sword, he stopped holding his stomach wound so tightly and thick liquid oozed out.

I raised my sword high over my right shoulder, ready to strike. I looked down straight into the man's eyes, and saw that they were brown like a hare's. I could feel my hands tremble a little. I didn't know if I was going to swing my blade down or not.

A flash of silver flew past me and a sword pierced the man squarely in the chest. His face changed from pain to peace and I knew he was gone.

I looked round and saw Tyral come striding across the clearing.

"The first man you kill should be in battle," he said simply.

I could see the gold hammer of Thor on the hilt of the weapon he had so accurately thrown.

"You follow Odin," I said suddenly. "Why did you accept a sword with Thor's hammer?"

Tyral put one foot on the man's chest as he pulled out his sword. It made a squelching noise.

"It was payment from your father. Who would turn away such a payment? And who would turn away such a sword?" he said. "And anyway, who is Thor's father?"

We walked back to the rest of the men. Someone had stumbled on a young deer in the trees and had managed to kill it. It was small and scrawny, but everyone felt that the surprise catch was at least a good omen. The best of the meat was cut from its bones and taken with us for later.

We kept moving. It was late afternoon now and there was a thin drizzle from the clouds and a thin mist in the air.

The nearer the battlefield we got, the more dead things we saw. I say "things" because with some of them it was hard to recognize what they were. I saw two large ravens flapping up and down the side of an oak tree, fighting over a dirty grey rope that was wound around its trunk. As we got closer, I saw a body next to the tree and realized it wasn't rope.

"Someone decided he was a coward or a traitor,"

said Harald the Thread. "He's been disembowelled." Disembowelled meant that as punishment his stomach had been slit open and his guts pulled out while he was still alive. One end of his intestine had been nailed to a tree and he had been forced to walk round and round the tree pulling out his own entrails as he went.

Harald the Thread saw me looking back at the two birds fighting as we walked past.

"The raven goes forth in the blood of those fallen in battle," he said, looking up at the banner he was holding. "He flies from the field of battle with blood on his beak, human flesh in his talons, and the reek of corpses on his breath."

I think that he was quoting from a poem, but I wanted him to stop talking because behind his words I could hear something. I knew what it was. Behind Harald the Thread talking about death, I could hear the sound of death itself.

The men fell silent. There was a loud cry of pain from the distance and every one of us tensed up. Hands moved towards swords.

The pathway we'd been following twisted around the tree line and then the battlefield came into view. Two rolling green hillsides led down to the battlefield and I saw now why we had taken such a long route to walk here. We were at the top of one of those slopes with the advantage of height on our side. At the bottom of the slope opposite were the ruins of monastery.

The battlefield was dark and muddy and was already strewn with the wounded and the dead. Looking at how many men I could see laying face down in the cold, wet, mud, it struck me that there would not be enough stories and songs in the whole world for them all to be remembered.

The noise was terrible. Metal swords hitting wooden shields, and swords hitting the metal of other swords. Men shouting to encourage their comrades, men shouting in pain, and worst of all, men calling out and being silenced forever as they died.

If Odin and his ravens lived for war and death and blood, then the scene in front of me was everything they could have wished for. Men slaughtering men in a mudbath of blood and bodies.

"Aggggggggggh!"

To the side of our band, two Scots warriors were suddenly charging towards us, their swords raised above their heads. I opened my mouth to shout a warning to Father and the others when a hail of half a dozen arrows hit the men. I looked round to see six of our archers, drawing back another arrow each, ready to fire.

Perhaps we were not as disorganized as I felt.

Two more warriors ran at us from the side, but before the archers could act, Tyral stepped forward from the group. As they ran straight at him, he sidestepped them both with the gentlest of movements and with a single sword stroke, cut open their guts as they passed him.

Seeing how well everyone else fought I became convinced I was going to die. I glanced over at Ragnar and he looked just as surprised and worried as I felt.

Tyral must have seen our reactions because he looked at us both and said: "Take your courage in your hands and fight. All we can do is live with honour."

I nodded although at that point I wasn't expecting to live for long, either with or without honour.

"Shieldwall!"

A shieldwall was the usual way our people fought. We had practised it every day in battle-training before we left. Every warrior faced the front and overlapped his shield with the shield of the man next to him. The idea was that you make a long unbreakable wall that no enemy could get through.

Everyone had to stay exactly in line though. If you moved forwards or backwards even a few steps and broke the line, then you'd probably not only get yourself killed, but everyone near you in the wall.

The best warriors went at the front in the shieldwall, and that wasn't us. We followed behind as the shieldwall raced down the slope. Our target was a group of Scots warriors who were moving in on a much smaller group who I took to be on our side. The battlefield was the most confusing and chaotic place I had ever seen and it was very hard to tell what was going on.

The Scots heard us coming of course. A few of them

turned to face us, but most of them didn't and our shieldwall smashed through their ranks. Many of them were knocked to the ground and some of them received fatal sword wounds from our leading warriors.

Ragnar was running down the slope ahead of me and I saw him swing his sword and strike a powerful blow at a man just climbing to his feet. He had made his first kill.

I stopped by another fallen man. As I raised my sword high over my right shoulder ready to strike, I saw he had dropped his sword as he'd fallen. I looked down, but I didn't look in his eyes. I could feel my hands tremble a little, then I brought my sword down as hard as I could with a single blow.

I ran on after Ragnar and the others. The shieldwall had got down the entire slope unbroken, but now there was no single group to aim a charge at so it split up and our men entered the battle where they were needed.

One of the enemy staggered towards me, swinging his sword wildly. Although we had been walking all day, we were fresh to the battlefield and many of these men were exhausted, or wounded, or both. My shield took the blow straight on, and I struck with my own sword. He was too slow to defend himself and fell.

We were near the bottom of the other slope now where the ruins of a monastery and its outbuildings sat crumbling to nothing. Ragnar was exchanging shield blows with one of the enemy when the man suddenly turned and ran off, following an overgrown path into the monastery. Ragnar gave chase and disappeared. Even then I knew it was a bad move.

I ran after him. As I turned down the path, several arrows from enemy archers flew past, just missing me. The enemy must have had men in some of the old buildings. Other warriors from our side entered the ruins now as the battle spilled away from the open field.

"Ragnar!"

I called his name, but there was no answer. I ran along the side of one of the grey stone buildings, trying to keep low in case there were more archers hiding in the ruins.

The building had long thin slits for windows and I caught a glimpse of Ragnar inside. I ran along, looking for the doorway Ragnar must have used, but at the next corner found that part of the wall and roof had collapsed, making a small hole. I scrambled up the wall and looked inside.

There were three keen warriors backing Ragnar into a corner. Three swords against one. As he retreated he got nearer to me. The hole in the roof was just big enough for him to climb though, but with three of the enemy just behind him I knew he would never make it out alive.

I had to save him. I had to try. So I pushed my legs over the sharp grey stones and jumped down inside.

Ragnar and I looked at each other very quickly. There was no need to say anything because we both understood.

The building was the old church and it felt cold and damp and had obviously been deserted for a long time. There were weeds sprouting from the floor and moss growing on some of the walls. It smelt of the dark and I didn't want to die there, even though that was what was going to happen.

One of the warriors said something to the others in a language that I couldn't understand. They were young like us.

The one nearest me struck a blow with his sword, making me raise my shield. One of the others did the same to Ragnar, but as he raised his shield the third struck with his sword against Ragnar's sword. He twisted his sword to get the better leverage and forced Ragnar's sword out of his hand and clattering on to the floor.

Now we had two shields and one sword against three shields and three swords and we both knew that we were dead and that we would never see mother or Flagg or climb the cliff for gulls' eggs again.

I thought about passing my sword to Ragnar as he probably had the better chance of killing one of them, but it was too risky.

The one who had forced Ragnar's sword out of his hand, stepped forward to strike again, and suddenly his eyes widened as he looked behind us. Something small and black and metal hit him in the shoulder. As he staggered back, I saw it was an arrowhead that had been thrown by hand.

"Ha – there you are."

It was Tyral. The hole was too small for him to climb through, but he had other ideas.

"Catch."

Tyral threw down the sword Father had given him. It fell through the air handle first and in one smooth perfect movement Ragnar caught it and swung it to face the enemy. Perhaps we would climb the cliff for gulls' eggs again.

Ragnar and I smiled at each other.

I thrust towards the enemy nearest me, aiming for his shield. But I was stupid. He stepped away from the force of the blow and my sword swung past his shield and into thin air. He got the timing just right, and brought his own sword down from high over his shoulder.

The last thing I remember seeing was the flash of grey metal on my sword arm and the sight of my severed hand falling to the floor.

The story of how there are some things that even the gods can't change

After that, I don't really know what happened because my memories are all mixed up.

I remember lots of faces looking down at me. They looked like they were looking at something extremely interesting, but at the same time really horrible. I remember being carried on someone's shoulder. As they ran, the hard bone pressed up hard into my ribs and it hurt.

I remember the person spinning around and I saw the face of one of the enemy warriors. He looked at me with a surprised expression, and then spots of dark red blood came from somewhere and hit his face. He raised his sword to strike at us, but whoever was carrying me was quicker. We spun around again and the man fell out of my vision. I never saw him again.

I remember someone placing me down on the ground. I lay there and it was cold and wet. Someone tried to make me drink water from a bowl, but I spat it out. It dribbled down my chin and made me colder still. I think I must have started shivering because someone wrapped a cloak around me. My arm felt like it was burning.

I heard the sound of the sea. Waves hitting rocks. Someone kept telling me to wake up and that we were nearly there, but I wanted to listen to the sea and more than anything I wanted to go to sleep.

Balder was the most handsome, and the most loved, and the happiest of all the gods, but he had become convinced that something terrible was going to happen to him.

Night after night he tossed and turned in bed as he suffered terrible dreams. In his nightmares, he was surrounded by dark formless shapes who wished him only harm.

Soon all the gods met to discuss Balder's troubles including his father, Odin, and his mother, Frigga.

"My brother, Balder, is so popular," said Thor, "I cannot imagine anyone wishing him harm."

All the gods nodded. Secretly, they each thought that if anything happened to Balder it could mean the beginning of the end for all the gods. Though they never admitted it, they were all worried.

"I will travel to the underworld and speak to Hel myself," said Odin. "I'll make sure that she has no plans to call Balder and then we can rest easy again."

Odin the Wise mounted Sleipnir, his eight-legged horse, and began the long, gloomy journey down into the land of the dead. When he got to Hel's great hall he entered and was surprised to find it decked out ready for a great feast.

"Who are you expecting?" said Odin to a servant.

"We are preparing a feast to welcome Balder, the son of Odin, to the land of the dead," said the servant, his skin grey and his eyes dull and lifeless.

Odin mounted his horse and returned to Asgard as quickly as he could, where the gods waited. When she heard the news, Frigga decided that the only way to protect her son was to travel through all the worlds and make every animal, every illness and every object swear an oath to never harm Balder. To a mortal, this would be an impossible task, but Frigga had not been Odin's wife for centuries without learning a trick or two. And so she embarked on her journey and was soon back from her mission.

"Everything that exists has sworn the oath, so Balder is safe," announced Frigga.

Thor thought that perhaps they should test this and threw a small stone at Balder. It bounced off his brother without hurting him at all. Balder was soon giving all the gods great sport by letting them attack him with any object they chose. Nothing hurt Balder at all.

The gods went back to their great halls and they were happy and content. All the gods that is except Loki. He hated the fuss that everyone always made of Balder just because he was good looking. A plan began to form in Loki's dark and twisted mind.

The next day, when Frigga was watching the gods testing Balder again, an ugly old woman hobbled up to Frigga.

"Why are the gods stoning that poor man?" asked the old woman.

Frigga moved away a step because the women smelt as if she had not washed for several moons.

"They're not stoning him. He's my son, and every animal, every illness and every object in the nine worlds has sworn not to hurt him," explained Frigga proudly.

"Everything?" said the old woman.

"Everything. Well, everything except that mistletoe bush on the oak tree. That's too small to ever hurt anyone," said Frigga, turning around to see that the old woman had disappeared.

Once she was out of sight, the old woman muttered a magical charm to herself and her form changed back into the shape-shifter, Loki. He had a smile on his twisted scarred lips.

The next day, the gods were once again testing Balder's invulnerability, this time with swords and arrows and spears.

Loki crept up to the back of the crowd where Balder's brother, Hod, stood alone.

"I know that you are blind," said Loki, "but it's not

fair of the others to stop you joining in. Here – I have something for you to throw at Balder and I will aim your arm as well."

"The others do not speak well of you, but you're very kind," said Hod, letting the trickster guide his arm.

The mistletoe arrow flew through the air and went straight through Balder's chest, splitting his heart in two. All eyes turned to look at Hod.

"What?" he said. "What has happened?"

Before Balder's dead body could hit the ground, Loki had vanished.

I woke up because someone was touching my arm and it really hurt. I tried to make them stop, but someone else held me down. I could still hear the sea. There were lots of faces looking down. I remember Tyral with his shoulder covered in blood. I was worried in case he'd been wounded, but when I tried to speak my lips wouldn't work.

I remember Harald the Thread leaning down close to my face. He stood up and embraced Father like he was saying goodbye, then he disappeared into the forest.

The next thing I remember is seawater splashing on my face. Once again I was being carried on someone's shoulder as they waded through the cold waves towards our longboat.

I woke up and there were more faces looking down. I woke up again and there was a dragon in the sky. Tyral was sitting by my side on the deck and he was leaning down, talking to me. Behind him I could see sweeping grey clouds moving across the sky. One was in the shape of a dragon. A perfect dragon. I could see the face, nose, ears, long neck, body, wings. A dragon in the sky.

I wanted to make Tyral look up so he could see the dragon as well, but he just kept talking, kept stopping me from going to sleep.

Balder's lifeless body lay on the floor surrounded by all the swords, stones and spears that everyone had thrown at him to test his invulnerability. The gods looked at Balder, then one by one they began to cry and wail so loudly that their sobs were heard throughout all the nine worlds.

The loudest crying came from Balder's mother, Frigga. "Who will ride to the land of the dead and see if Hel will accept any ransom to release my precious Balder?" she asked.

The gods shifted uneasily because it was a terrible journey full of many dark dangers, and although they loved Balder, no one wanted to undertake it.

"I will go," said Hermodur. "I will go and try to free my brother."

Odin gave Hermodur his mighty eight-legged horse, and Hermodur galloped away into the gloom.

The rest of the gods carried Balder's body down to the edge of the ocean and put him on board his great longship, Ringhorn. Nanna, who was Balder's wife, looked at his face and saw that it was dull and grey, and that all the shining brightness had left it. Her heart broke and she fell down dead on top of him.

The gods wept as they built a huge pyre on the ship with all Balder's belongings. Odin leaned over his son and whispered a secret word into his ear. Then he placed Draupnir, the magical ring that produced eight more rings every ninth night, with Balder on the boat.

The burial shore was crowded with gods, and rock giants, and frost giants, and trolls, and elves, and even dwarfs, who stood blinking in the light of the setting sun.

The gods asked the giantess Hyrrokin to push the boat out to sea. She gave it such a shove that the ship and the rollers it was running over burst into flames. The most powerful gods in all the worlds stood helpless and weeping as the boat sailed out to sea in a blaze of fire. It got lower and lower in the water until, just as it met the setting sun, it sank beneath the waves.

"We must hope Hermodur is both swift and successful," said Odin, but there was very little hope in his voice.

Even as Balder's ship was sinking beneath the waves,

Hermodur was riding down and down and down into the underworld. For nine nights he rode until eventually he came to the dark realm of the dead ruled over by Loki's daughter, Hel. He entered the great hall where in the middle of a thousand thousand corpses he saw Balder, pale and drawn, sitting in the seat of honour. The corpses nearest Balder had each placed a cold, dead hand upon him.

Hermodur approached Hel and tried not to look at the part of her flesh that was dead and rotten with crawling maggots. "I come to ask on behalf of all of the gods if you will release Balder the Brave and allow him to return to the land of the living," he said, striving to keep his voice from shaking.

"Nobody ever leaves this place," whispered Hel.

"But Balder was like a bright light in the centre of Asgard," insisted Hermodur. "Every creature in the nine worlds weeps for Balder."

"All right then," said Hel. "If every single creature really does weep for him, every god, every giant and every man, then I will release him. But if there is a single being that does not shed a tear, he stays here forever."

Hermodur knew he would not get a better deal from Hel so he rode back to Asgard as quickly as he could, spreading the word. Soon every god, dwarf and mortal man – even every troll – wept for Balder.

Down in the underworld, the corpses holding Balder released their grip one by one by one until there was just one dead hand gripping Balder and keeping him trapped in the hall of the dead. The gods rode far and wide across all the lands to see who was not weeping for Balder.

Hermodur found an old and ugly giantess named Thokk sitting in her cave. The more he asked her, the more she refused to cry for the dead man.

"I care nothing for Balder," she said with a snarl. "Let Hel keep what she has."

The news was taken back to Asgard. Many people expected the gods to rise up in anger and force the old giantess to cry for Balder. But they did not. Odin's eyes filled with tears again and, looking older, he just shuffled away into the permanent twilight that had settled on Asgard.

After a while, the giants realized that none of them knew of a giantess called Thokk. When they went to pay her a visit, they found her cave empty and deserted. After that, no one doubted that the old giantess was really Loki the shape-changer.

Next time I woke up I was in a bed. There were more faces looking down at me and I didn't recognize any of them. I was in a house made of grey stone, like many I'd seen on the islands we had sailed past. I was hot. Too hot. I could hear the sound of water dripping into a bowl. A woman was putting a cloth into a bowl of water and then putting the moist material on my forehead. The cloth was cool.

From across the room I could hear Father praying to Odin. The bed was wet with sweat and even though the water was cold, I was still hot. There was the sound of water dripping into a bowl. A woman was putting a cloth into a bowl of water and then putting it on my forehead. It was cool, but I was still too hot. My hand hurt.

Hanging on the wall above my head was a shield. It was battered, and there were bits missing in places, where it had taken blows from a sword. The shield had a green background with two dark-green wolves on it. The wolves had a bright white eyes and fangs like ice. It was my shield.

I wanted to tell someone that it was my shield on the wall, but I was too hot. There was the sound of water dripping into a bowl and a woman put a cloth on my forehead. It was cool.

Sometimes the faces looking down at me changed, but I was still too hot.

After Balder had to stay in the underworld Loki, the master of lies, knew that he was living on borrowed time. He was certain that Odin, Thor and all the other gods would want to take revenge on him.

So Loki left Asgard for the last time and fled far

away. For the first time in his long life he was scared. He went to the tallest, coldest, least hospitable mountain he could find, and there he built a small stone hut with a door in each of the four walls so he could keep watch in every direction. But still Loki could not sleep easy and spent all day and all night thinking how he could hide himself better.

There was a river near his hut where each morning he would change into a salmon. There he would spend the day hidden in the white water at the base of a waterfall called Franang's Falls. Yet even as he swam there, thoughts of how the gods might catch a salmon began to fill Loki's mind. One evening as he sat alone by his small fire, he played with some lengths of twine to see how easy it might be for them to make a net.

The next morning at dawn, Loki woke with a start. There were voices coming up the valley. He threw the half-made net into the smouldering fire and ran to the river, changing into a salmon as he jumped in.

Loki was right to flee because it was the voices of a party of gods he had heard. Odin could see everything in all the nine worlds, and it was only a matter of time before he found Loki. The gods burst into Loki's cold, damp hut, one entering through each of his four doors.

"He's not here, but he was," said Thor. "Let us carry on the search."

"One moment," said Kvasir, looking down at the fire where he saw the burnt remains of the fishing net, its pattern left clearly as grey ash. "See this? Let us make our own net and go fishing."

The gods sat by the river and made a net, while Loki swam backwards and forwards, backwards and forwards in the watery depths.

When the net was ready, the gods approached the river. The first time they trawled the water, Loki swam right to the bottom and slipped under the net. So the gods attached weights to the mesh. The second time the gods trawled the river, Loki suddenly leapt from the water and over the net. But the third time they trawled the river, the gods were ready for him. For once, Loki was out of tricks. When he leapt over the net, Thor grabbed hold of the slippery salmon and did not let go.

The gods stood around watching the fish thrash about on the riverbank until Loki had to change back into human form or die. The prince of lies was trapped at last.

"Stand up," said Thor. "You are to be punished."

Although it would give them little pleasure, the gods knew what they had to do next.

When I woke up, Mother was looking down at me. At first I thought it must be someone else who looked like her, but when I opened my eyes again it was still Mother.

Someone sat me up and I had to drink a cup of brew that tasted of bitter herbs. They wouldn't let me lie down again until I had nearly finished the cupful. My hand hurt.

I saw Magnus looking down at me. He looked exactly the same as when we left. He stood at the end of the bed and kept making the sign of a healing rune, a kind of magical letter, in the air, and chanting to Odin, chanting to Odin, chanting to Odin.

I woke up. It was night and my hand hurt and everyone was asleep apart from Mother, who was sitting next to me in a chair. She put a piece of cloth in a bowl of water and then placed it on my forehead, and then she smiled at me.

My hand still hurt, but I could feel my fingers now and under the bed covers I moved them just a little.

The gods had caught Loki and now they had to punish him. They knew that the punishment had to be terrible and that it would make Loki hate them forever. For the next time they were to see Loki would be at Ragnarok, the Doom of the Gods, when he would lead the forces of darkness against them.

First the gods found Loki's two sons. They whispered a magic rune-word which changed one into a wolf. He leapt on his brother, ripping open his body. The gods took out the boy's intestines, then carried Loki to the deep, dark cave where Thokk had refused to weep for Balder.

The gods tied Loki to three rocks, using his own son's intestines as his bonds. The dripping entrails instantly became as hard as iron and he was completely helpless. But the gods weren't finished yet. They caught a snake that was heavy with venom and tied it to a stalactite so that it hung just above Loki, hissing and spitting its poison into his face. Then the gods sealed the cave behind them and left Loki inside, tormented and alone in the dark forever.

But the old trickster wasn't quite alone. Out of love, his wife, Sigyn, had asked to remain with him. She stayed to hold a bowl between Loki and the snake, to collect the venom that would otherwise fall on to his face. When the bowl became full, she had to turn to empty it. In those moments, the venom dropped on Loki, making him scream and struggle against his bonds. Whenever that happened, the earth itself shook somewhere in the world of men.

The gods returned to Asgard with heavy hearts. They wished that things were different. They wished that Balder was still alive. They wished that Loki was a mischief-making friend instead of a bitter, resentful enemy. They wished that Ragnarok, the Doom of the Gods, did not seem so close. And most of all they wished that they felt young again instead of old and weary. But they knew that there are some things that even the gods cannot change.

I woke up and I heard Magnus's voice telling a story. I think he had been telling it while I was asleep because I don't remember hearing the beginning. I looked down the bed and at the end I saw Magnus on one side and Ragnar on the other. My hand ached.

"Hello," I said.

"Tor!" said Ragnar.

They both looked surprised to see me, as if they hadn't known I was there.

"How do you feel?" said Magnus.

I felt like the cliff top when it's been hot and humid for days. Then there is a great thunderstorm and afterwards the air smells clean and fresh.

"I feel hungry," I answered.

Magnus waved a hand and said, "I must get your mother." He left me with Ragnar.

"I had strange dreams that we went somewhere to fight," I said.

Ragnar suddenly looked upset.

"I want you to have this," he said, lifting up a magnificent sword with a gold hammer in the hilt. It was Tyral's sword.

"You can train with it," he said. "Start again."

"But that's Tyral's sword," I said. "I can't have it."

The thought of holding that heavy sword made my right hand hurt. My left arm was free, but my right arm was tucked tightly under the bed covers.

"After, you know ... what happened, Tyral gave it to me," said Ragnar. "But I don't want it. I want you to have it. It's yours. I know you wanted it."

I wriggled the fingers of my right hand under the bed covers.

"Help me," I said, trying to get my arm free.

"You were very brave," said Ragnar for no reason that I could understand, and his eyes filled up with tears. "Everyone thought you were going to die on the boat."

Ragnar didn't help me, but it didn't matter because my arm was free now.

"I'm so sorry," said Ragnar.

I looked down. I had felt my fingers moving, making and unmaking a fist. But now I could see that my right arm ended at the wrist.

My hand wasn't there. It was completely gone.

The story of the end

"I want you to hit me as hard as you can," said Ragnar, looking me straight in the eye.

We were on the cliff where you can see out to the ocean, but the village can't see you. The trees in the forest behind us were already shedding their leaves for autumn. I raised my sword and brought it down on Ragnar's shield. I nearly missed completely. Ragnar had to push his shield into my sword to make it sound like a proper blow.

"That was better," he said.

It wasn't.

I was trying to train holding my sword in my left hand and it wasn't going well. It hadn't been going well all week. I'd never been a brilliant swordsman with my right hand, but with my weaker left hand it was hopeless.

Everyone said I'd been very brave on the raid and that climbing into the ruined church to fight had saved Ragnar's life. I didn't remember much about it. I remembered running downhill following the shieldwall, but everything after that was a jumble.

I was sad to hear that Tyral had left the village while I

was still in bed with fever. Of course, it was Tyral who had carried me on his shoulder through the forest and to the ship. I wanted to thank him for saving my life, and for many other things besides.

"He waited as long as he could," explained Ragnar. "But he didn't want the weather to turn bad for his voyage home, so he had to go."

Tyral said he was going to his home village to settle up his business and then he was going to return. Not even Ragnar believed he was really coming back, but I knew he would. If Tyral made up his mind to do something then he did it. I often thought of the night on the ship when he had whispered to me the story of Loki's monstrous children. Whenever I told that story now, I did it just like he had.

Sometimes, as the evenings got longer and we sat around the fire, I would watch the flames reflected in the twisted, hardened skin where my arm ended at the wrist. In my dreams, I always had two hands. It was strange to wake up each morning and remember one was gone. Especially as I could sometimes feel my fingers moving as if they were still there.

There's a saying among our people: "A corpse is no good to anyone, but even a handless man can herd sheep." I think it was supposed to mean that as long as you weren't dead, you could do something useful in the village. I didn't want to herd sheep though. And it was obvious (at least to me) that there was no point in me training to fight. I'd never be a warrior. I wasn't even sure I wanted to be one any more, although I still enjoyed hearing and telling the stories of the gods slaying giants and trolls. Not that I said that aloud to anyone.

I stopped training with Ragnar in the afternoons, although we were still best friends. He had completely forgiven me for that stupid fight. He just kept saying that I had saved his life in the battle, although I couldn't quite put the pieces together that way in my head.

While Ragnar was training I spent more time with Magnus. He told me more stories and he taught me about the runes. He told me how the great All-Father himself, Odin, had approached the spring of Mimir so thirsty for knowledge that he was willing to pluck out one of his own eyes for a single drink from the well of wisdom. Although that drink allowed Odin to gain great insight, it only made him want more.

So Odin travelled to Yggdrasill, the ancient tree at the centre of the worlds, where he hung in agony for nine long and lonely nights from one of the trees branches. Odin pierced his own side with a spear and, because there was no higher being in any world, he offered himself to himself as a sacrifice. He died so he could learn the secrets of the dead and then he returned to life so he could use those secrets.

The knowledge he brought back with him from that dark place were nine songs full of wisdom and eighteen runes.

The runes were magical letters full of power. They could be used to record things, keep a calendar or send messages. You could also use runes to cast magical spells to help people, as Magnus had done to help get rid of my fever. Used correctly by someone who knew their magic, the runes could heal the sick, blunt an enemy's weapon, put out fire, seduce a lover, calm a storm, and even allow the user to speak to the dead.

Magnus now spoke to me like I was a man instead of a boy. I didn't know if it was because I had been away to fight, or if it was because these days I did more listening and less asking questions. I went with Sven the Silent into the forest on his trips to collect leaves and herbs to make potions. I found out that he was not so much silent as softly spoken.

Winter came fast. One morning it was warm enough to wander out of the longhouse on to the soft grass without my shoes, and the next there was a cold, crunchy frost under my feet. There was suddenly a lot of work to do and everyone pulled together to do it, as always.

People sent their slaves to cut grass in the pastures so it could be dried to make hay to feed livestock. Then animals were brought down from the upper pastures. The weakest ones were killed and the women had the job of making sure that the meat would keep over the whole winter.

To do this they started boiling large cauldrons full of seawater. They kept the cauldrons over a fire until all the liquid boiled away, leaving white salt crystals at the bottom.

They had to do it again and again to get as much salt as they needed.

The slaughtered animals were sliced up and the pieces of meat packed into barrels with a layer of salt on each of them. The salt stopped the meat going rotten. When they were full, the barrels were moved to one of the unheated storehouses where no one lived.

There were five large longhouses in the village, and everyone crowded into them for the winter. Even Magnus came down from his hut in the forest where he lived the rest of the year. There was always a large fire burning, partly to keep us warm and partly so the women could cook. It was very smoky inside, which meant that most of us had a cough until spring.

At the end of each longhouse there was an area fenced off where we kept the animals. That part had to have a sloping floor so that their mess ran away outside. It wasn't too bad having the animals inside because at least they helped make the place warmer.

There weren't as many animals to look after as usual. Sigund the Bloody said that Old One Ear the wolf had eaten more lambs this year than were born, and he wasn't far wrong. He was busy moving the animals and also looking after Harald the Thread's widow, Gudrid, who was now very large with child.

Harald the Thread had been killed during the battle. He had died a hero's death being struck by fifty enemy arrows, although the story changed depending on who was telling it. Sometimes stories do that – usually they get bigger and more detailed, but this one just changed. I wanted to ask many questions, but I knew it wasn't the time.

The nights soon became long and dark and cold. The sun became weaker until it only just managed to creep over the horizon around midday and even then it had little heat in it. It snowed most days.

Inside the longhouse, the children ran and screamed and played and got on the adults' nerves. The adults played dice games and chess and got on each other's nerves. The cattle broke wind several times a day and got on everyone's nerves.

When people ventured outside into the cold, they used ice legs made of horse bone, tied to the bottom of their leather shoes, to slide over the frozen ground, pushing themselves along with a pointed iron pole across the ice and snow. It was the best way of getting around in winter and the children loved to use them on the frozen river when the ice was thick enough.

The Yule feast was coming up so Ragnar and I went hunting on the upper slopes. There was not enough daylight to go deep into the forest so we lay hidden in the thick snow by a rabbit warren on the pasture, waiting for any unwary rabbits that might emerge.

Ragnar had told me the story of Harald the Thread's death and now felt like a good time to ask him about it again.

"It is a great shame about Harald the Thread," I said.

"Ssssh," said Ragnar.

"Did he die well?"

Ragnar squinted down the rabbit hole. "He was a hero. He saved Father by stepping in the way of sixty or seventy poison-tipped arrows," he said.

This was the first I had heard that the fifty, sixty or seventy arrows were also poison-tipped.

"The only thing is..." I said.

"Ssssh. I think I see a rabbit," said Ragnar.

"The only thing is, I think I remember Harald saying goodbye to Father when we were on our way back to the ship."

Ragnar looked at me. "I *thought* you saw him when he leaned down to say goodbye to you." Then he whispered urgently, "You can't tell anyone, on our blood oath. Only a few of us know. Harald didn't want to come home, so he jumped ship to go to Iceland."

"But his wife is having a..."

I never finished because suddenly it all made sense.

And in the middle of the afternoon you could see Harald the Thread's wife, Gudrid, sneak away from her washing duty at the river, walk round the edge of the village and duck into the woods. At the same time on the other side of the village, Sigund the Bloody would leave the cows he was supposed to be tending and also disappear into the woods.

Two rabbits, noses twitching in the cold air, had emerged

from the darkness of the tunnel. With perfect aim, Ragnar threw his sword and speared one through the leg. I'd told him about Tyral throwing his sword at the injured man in the forest before the battle and I think Ragnar had been practising.

By the time we went back we had five rabbits between us.

We always celebrate mid-winter and the shortest day of the year with a huge Yule feast. We don't actually celebrate the shortest day, but rather the fact that it has passed. The wheel of the year was turning and from now on the days would gradually get longer and warmer until spring. But there was still the rest of winter to survive.

Ten days after the Yule feast ended, everyone in our longhouse was woken up in the night by a scream. Sometimes I had nightmares about the battle I had seen, but this was not a dream. Gudrid's baby was coming.

The women moved her into a side room and everyone else paced around and waited. Sven the Silent prepared brews to drink and the women took them to her. As the day passed, I could tell from the tone in Mother's voice that she was getting anxious. Mother even called Magnus into the room at one point. When he came out he looked very serious, and I knew we were going to do something.

Magnus got dressed to go out into the cold and so did I. The collar on my cloak was loose because I kept forgetting to ask Mother to fix it and Magnus looked at it disapprovingly.

"Do you remember in the spring, Asgot the Green had a goat that wouldn't give birth even though it was more than her time?" he said, pulling on a thick woollen cape. "We gave her a herb brew. Now we need the same for Gudrid."

"She's not a goat," I said.

"Her baby is a baby and Gudrid needs what she needs," said Magnus, wrapping a fur around the cape.

Magnus grabbed his long wooden staff. It had runes carved all the way down its bark and wherever Magnus left it you could be sure that no one else would ever touch it.

We opened the longhouse's thick wooden door and an icy blast blew in. Voices shouted in cold complaint, and we stepped outside quickly, holding the door open just long enough for Flagg to follow.

"*Caw!*"

Flagg acted as if he'd just been let out of a cage, which I suppose he had.

"I have the plant leaves we need in my home," said Magnus. "We must be quick." He always referred to his shaky, draughty wooden shack on the edge of the forest as "home" even though he spent much of the year in the longhouse with the rest of us.

We set off through the snow, a boy with one hand, and an old man with legs as thin as a cow's tail. Flagg hopped and flew with us. His claws looked like wrinkled maggots and when they got too cold in the snow he settled on Magnus's shoulder. He never sat on anyone else's.

The snow slowed our journey to the hut. When we reached it, Magnus disappeared inside. I wasn't invited. When he came out, he was frowning and holding a small wooden box. It was open, and I could see what looked like green ash inside.

"Eaten by insects," said Magnus.

He moved away from the long shadow of the hut and looked at the sun. It never got very high in the sky in winter and much of its light was cut out by the forest.

I knew what Magnus was thinking. He knew where in the forest the plant grew. I felt my pocket and made sure I could feel the shape of my small knife. It would cut through a branch or thick bark if we needed it to.

If Magnus decided to do something, he always did it. You could wager your best sword on it.

"We can make it. There's plenty of light. It won't be dark for a long time," I said, which wasn't true at all and Magnus knew it.

"You're right," he said.

We found the path, which in itself wasn't easy, and followed it into the trees.

Once the trees closed behind us, the crashing of the sea on the cliffs faded away. The forest was still and silent. Nothing was moving. Every tree had a coating of silver frost. Little crystals of ice hung everywhere.

The only noise was the sound of our footsteps. However

softly we tried to walk, the frost and ice cracked like the spit of a fire under our feet.

There was no movement anywhere. No birdsong. Nothing. It made me feel like we were intruding into the end of the world.

"This must be what Ragnarok looks like," I whispered to Magnus.

Ragnarok, the Doom of the Gods and the end of the world.

"Hail to the speaker and hail to the listener!" said Magnus, breaking the silent spell that the icy forest had spun over us both.

"*Caw!*"

Flagg flapped from Magnus's shoulder into a tree.

"May whoever hears and learns these words prosper because of them. Hail to those who listen," intoned Magnus, raising his arms to the trees.

"In the end," he boomed loudly, "there will be only two things – fire and ice."

We walked and Magnus talked.

"Ragnarok begins when war spreads across the earth to the corners of every land. Brother will fight his brother and fathers will kill their sons. Blood will wash through the world like rain. Then after the war will come the winter of all winters."

"Colder than even this?" I said, because I knew Magnus liked it when people said things like that.

"This will seem like summer compared to Fimbulvetr,

the terrible winter before Ragnarok. Snow and ice will hold the world of men in its freezing grip, and three winters will follow each other with no summer in between."

Magnus knew how to make a cold journey pass.

"In the sky, Skoll the wolf will eat the sun and the world will be plunged into total darkness. On earth, terrible earthquakes will shake and shatter the land. All chains will be broken, including the strongest chain of all, the one holding Fenris the wolf. Knowing that the end is near, the Midgard Serpent will wake and begin to move, twisting and writhing towards the shore. The thrashing of his enormous body will create terrible tidal waves that flood the land."

I helped Magnus over a fallen tree.

"On all of the stormy oceans of the world, only one ship will sail. That ship will be Naglfar, with the hull, decks and masts made from the nails of dead men. On board the ship will be an army of angry giants heading to Asgard for the final battle. At the helm of this dark ship will stand the third of Loki's children, Hel, freed at last from her gloomy world of the dead. Standing next to Hel, looking towards Asgard with hate-filled eyes, will be the father of lies himself, Loki."

We had reached a clearing. Magnus counted the trees on the edge and under the ninth tree began to dig away the snow.

"This plant grows better deeper in the forest, but this will do the job," he said.

Magnus was tired already from the walk and I took over

moving the snow. I might only have one hand, but I had more energy than he did.

"The gods will look at the forces gathered against them and they will know that they cannot escape their fate," continued Magnus once he'd caught his breath. "They will see Fenris the wolf with his mouth open so wide that his top jaw will scrape against the sky itself, while his bottom jaw will drag along the ground. They will watch the Midgard Serpent spew its poison far and wide across the sky. They will see the ship full of vengeful giants riding the rough waves. And they will see the turncoat Loki leading the attack."

Magnus pointed at the frozen, crushed plant I had uncovered and I got out my small knife and began cutting away leaves. The sun was sinking lower in the sky and it was getting even colder.

"On the rainbow bridge, Heimdall will blow his mighty horn and the gods will prepare for war. In Valhalla great warriors will pick up their swords and shields and prepare to ride with Odin to battle. As the forces meet on the battlefield, Odin the All-Father will head straight towards Fenris the wolf. Thor will stand ready to help his father, but he will be attacked by the Midgard Serpent. It will be the most terrible of battles, but by the end Thor will slay the great serpent. As the serpent dies, it will vomit venom over the thunder god. Thor will walk nine steps and then he too will die."

"*Caw!*"

Flagg flapped around under a tree at the edge of the clearing. He was making a fuss about being cold. I couldn't feel my fingers any more.

"Loki and Heimdall will fight with sword and shield until, at the same instant, each delivers a death blow to the other. After a terrible and bloody fight, Fenris the wolf will open his jaws as wide as the whole of existence and then he will swallow Odin. The other gods will rush forward and grab the jaws of the exhausted Fenris, pulling them apart, ripping the wolf in two."

I put the leaves in my pocket and felt them pressing cold and hard against me.

"CAW!"

Flagg was fidgeting. He suddenly flapped his one-and-a-half wings and flew off in an awkward zigzag flight. I had seen it before.

"Surt the fire demon will appear and will throw his gift of orange flame over all the lands. Niflheim, the home of the dead, Jotunheim, the home of the giants, Midgard, the home of men, and Asgard, the home of the gods. All of them will burn and be consumed by fire. Nothing will escape. No animal. No fish. No giant. No dwarf. No woman. No warrior. No god. Nothing," whispered Magnus.

I looked across the clearing and I felt a little sick in my stomach. A dark and monstrous shape was stalking silently out of the frozen trees.

It was Old One Ear the wolf.

"He looks hungry," I said, which was very true.

"Do you have the leaves?" said Magnus.

"Yes."

"Take my wooden staff and go," he said, pressing it into my hands.

"What?"

"Take my wooden staff and go. Take the leaves to your mother and don't look back whatever you hear," said Magnus, pushing himself slowly to his feet.

The wolf shifted forward. His dark shape was hard to see against the blackness of the trees behind.

"Go," Magnus hissed again, giving me a shove.

Magnus moved sideways around the edge of the clearing and away from me, and I saw what he meant to do.

I had the plant leaves in my pocket. I had the wooden staff. And I had the quicker legs. If I ran, I could probably save myself and the baby.

"*CAW!*"

Flagg flapped around above us, but the wolf had his eyes firmly fixed on Magnus.

I saw the old man's hand tremble. Just a bit. And I knew I could never leave him to a wolf.

I took out my knife and cut through the leather belt I was wearing. I had no time to untie it with one hand. Then I took the knife and put it at the end of the staff, and wrapped the belt around and around and around.

The wolf stepped nearer to Magnus.

I tried to tie a knot with my one hand and my foot. With my one hand and my mouth. With my one hand and anything.

Old One Ear was ready and I wasn't and I was too late. Suddenly Flagg dropped on to the face of the old wolf.

"*CAW! CAW!!*"

It was enough to buy me time. The wolf had black feathers in its mouth, but I saw that Flagg was away and flying. Magnus stumbled back and fell in the snow. The wolf, driven more by hunger than courage, stepped forward too quickly and on to the end of my small knife tied to the end of the old man's walking staff held in my one hand.

The blade pierced just above his left eye. The shock and the pain made him wince, and he turned and ran. His front paws slipped on the ice, he fell, got to his feet and disappeared into the trees.

He was gone.

I sat there in the snow until my heart stopped banging in my ears.

I sat there next to Magnus and we looked at each other.

Flagg landed on my shoulder and I saw he had grey wolf fur under his sharp talons.

"We'd best get back then," said Magnus.

We headed back home over snow and ice, and frozen rivers and fallen trees. I had never seen the old man move so quickly in all my life.

The story of the storyteller

The baby grew fat and she grew quickly. Everyone said it was a good sign for the village and that it meant the gods were pleased.

Magnus insisted that I should keep his wooden staff carved with runes that no one else ever touched. Together we added my name down one side.

The snows melted, the days warmed and the animals went back outside in the pastures where they could break wind without anyone complaining.

In the spring, Harald the Thread's "widow" Gudrid married Sigund the Bloody. A widow could marry whoever she wanted to and didn't need anybody's permission to do it. I thought about Harald the Thread and I hoped that wherever he was, far across the ocean, he was happier than he'd been in our village, where he would sometimes walk around muttering to himself.

Ragnar practised with his sword and I practised with my runes, and we stayed best friends.

One spring day, after the first of the yellow flowers were in bloom, but before the seabirds had laid their first batch of eggs on the cliff, a boat sailed up to our pier. Missionaries got out and began to talk to people about their one true god, the White Christ. When that happened, Father laid a long cloth over his shrine to Odin in the house to hide it and Magnus sneaked off to his hut.

Before he went, Magnus set me a task to find nine particular healing plants in bloom in the forest before dusk. Ragnar wanted to find good tree wood to fashion arrows with, so he came with me as far as the waterfall.

These days the forest was alive with birds and animals, making nests and digging holes and building dens ready for the arrival of their young. I followed the same path Magnus and I had taken that winter day before the baby came. I remembered how dead the forest had seemed then and how alive it was now.

As I walked I thought about what happens in the stories after the end of the world. After the gods are killed by the monsters and all the worlds burn in fire, a new green land will be born, when the land rises out of the ocean again and two humans who hid themselves away from the fire will emerge.

The two humans are a man called Lif and a woman called Lifthrasir, and the new land will give them food. Animals and birds and fish will appear, along with several of the young gods, and best of all Balder the Brave will return from the land of the dead to brighten the new world.

The Midgard Serpent made a complete circle by having its own tail in its mouth and so did the fate of the world. Just like the wheel of the year that was endlessly turning from hot to cold and from winter to spring to summer.

I saw one of the plants Magnus wanted me to find and it made me really smile. As I walked across the clearing towards the little bush, I saw a dark shape move in the corner of my eye.

It was the end of my story. I knew as soon as I saw the wolf that I had been careless and that now he would rip me apart with those teeth.

I was annoyed that I had been so stupid as to wander and chance upon the hungriest beast in the forest without even a sword. I had never meant to go so far.

Old One Ear the wolf took a step closer. He must have spent the rest of the winter hiding in the deep forest, and now there were young lambs again he was back. Just like last year.

I was in the middle of the clearing and had nowhere to run. I moved my wooden rune staff so that it was between my body and the wolf, and I held it tightly in my hand.

I thought of Ragnar and his sword with the golden hammer, but I had left him a long way behind by the waterfall.

I knew that One Ear would surely kill me and eat me right there. If only to stop me raising the alarm. If only because he hadn't been able to sink his sharp, glistening fangs into my flesh on that terrible day back in the frozen mid-winter when he had hunted me and Magnus in this same forest.

One Ear shifted his head from side to side. As he moved, I saw that there was something very wrong with his left eye. It was a wound about an inch across and flesh had healed over the eye, leaving it dead and useless. I wondered if he remembered me.

The wolf curved his old body, keeping his good eye fixed firmly on me. It was a hunting movement, and it reminded me that I was about to be eaten alive. If I turned and broke into a run, I knew the wolf would be on me and bring me down in seconds. I was a long way from the village or help.

I wanted to fight like Thor, but I had no mighty hammer. I wanted to struggle against this beast like Odin fighting Fenris at the end of days, but I knew that like him, I would lose.

I had no proper weapon again. I had my long staff of twisted wood, and if I could get it out in time, I had my small knife in my pocket for cutting plants. And, of course, I had just one hand to fight with. But this time I had no help.

What a pair we must have looked. Tor the Tale and Old One Ear. A boy of sixteen summers with a stump where his right hand should be, and a wolf with one ear and one eye.

Now I was near the end, I suddenly wondered what had happened to my hand, left so far away on a muddy battlefield, across the sea in another land. Had it been trampled by heavy leather boots and buried deep in mud? Or was it stripped to the bone by ravens with open-mouthed young to feed?

The old wolf took a step closer, bending his head down towards the ground. Not yet ready to leap, but nearly.

I carefully leaned the staff against my shoulder and moved my left hand towards the pocket where my knife was. I had it out now, hidden under my clothes so that it wouldn't catch the high midday sun and draw the wolf's attention.

In one quick sweep, I stepped forward and moved my staff so that it pointed towards One Ear like a blunt spear. The wolf snorted. My left hand held the knife low and out of sight. I had an idea of using the staff and stabbing with the knife, but then I saw again the size of his jaws and I knew this really was the end.

One Ear came a step forwards. I poked the staff. He moved back. Again he came forwards, and again I poked the staff towards him. He barely moved.

He was so close now that I could smell his breath. It smelt of rotting teeth, festering meat and death. It smelt like a battlefield.

His lips quivered, exposing sharp yellow daggers. His breath was heavy now. He was near the end of his life. But then, so was I now.

I suddenly got annoyed that this old wolf would be the finish of my story, instead of me being the end of his.

I saw his muscles tense up. He snarled. Then, in a burst of

movement and fury, and hatred and hunger, One Ear leapt towards me.

A flash of silver flew past me and a sword pierced the wolf squarely in the chest. His growl changed to a whimper in an instant and I knew he was gone. A pool of oozing red liquid flooded out from underneath him.

I looked round and saw Ragnar come striding across the clearing. I could see the gold hammer of Thor on the hilt of the weapon he had so accurately thrown.

"Are you all right?"

I hadn't realized I was on the ground, but Ragnar pulled me up to my feet thinking he was helping. My legs weren't ready to work yet and to his surprise I fell straight down again. Ragnar smiled at me, realizing his mistake, then we both saw that there was blood on my hand.

"Did he hurt you?"

While I had waited for the wolf to strike I had held my little knife so tightly I'd cut myself. I was no warrior.

Ragnar hauled me to my feet again. He was certainly keen to have company at the same height as him.

"Whoever kills the wolf will certainly have stories told about him." I smiled.

"We can say you did it. We can tell everyone you killed him," said Ragnar. And he meant it too.

"No," I said. "I'll tell the story … about how *you* killed him."

It took us most of the rest of the morning to skin the wolf.

He would make someone a fine coat. We worked in silence as the sun moved across the clear sky above us and warmed us through.

"You're a very good hunter," I said as we walked back towards the village. "You got very close to the wolf without him seeing you."

"I had help. As I got nearer, I could see he was practically blind in one eye, so I approached along that line where he couldn't see me."

Ragnar shifted the weight of the wolfskin from one shoulder to the other. "I'd guess that was your doing," he added, grinning.

When we got to the lookout point on the cliff I saw another new ship tied up at the pier. It had a black and white sail.

"Oh no, more missionaries," I said.

Ragnar was smiling.

"That's the ship that Tyral sailed away in," he said, looking at me.

We ran.

We ran downhill and through the village, and to the pier, and we didn't ever stop.

I had so many stories to tell.

Historical note

Dire portents appeared in the sky and sorely frightened the people. Immense whirlwinds and flashes of lightning, and fiery dragons were seen flying the air. A great famine immediately followed those signs, and a little after that on 8 June, the ravages of heathen men miserably destroyed God's church on Lindisfarne, with plunder and slaughter.
The Anglo-Saxon Chronicle AD 793

One summer's day in AD 793, monks living in the monastery on Lindisfarne, a small island off the north-east coast of England, looked out to sea watching storm clouds hanging low over the ocean. Suddenly they saw a fleet of dark ships appear over the horizon, speeding towards their holy island. The intruders landed their longships on the beach and rushed to the monastery with swords in hand.

According to records the intruders then "laid all waste with dreadful havoc, dug up the alters and carried off all the treasures of the holy church. Some of the monks they killed; some they carried off in chains; many they cast out naked and loaded with insults; some they drowned at sea".

The savage raid on the undefended and unarmed monastery sent shock waves across Europe. Monasteries were not defended because no one would ever dare to attack them. The Vikings that ransacked Lindisfarne clearly hadn't read the rule book. The raid marked the beginning of over 250 years of Viking raids, robbery, looting, pillage and occupation.

No one is quite sure where the name Viking originally came from. It might have come from the word "vik" which is Norse for a "bay on the sea" or it might have come from the word "vikja" which meant "to move quickly". Their victims soon understood that the word "vikingr" meant a pirate and to go "viking" meant to go on a raid.

Seeing the success of the early raids, more Vikings began to follow suit, sailing their longboats along the coasts of France, Germany, Ireland, Italy and the rest of Europe. They took whatever treasure they could find and also captured people to take home and either use or sell as slaves.

The Vikings were known as "the terror of the north" and it is easy to understand why. As Tor explains in the story, the Viking longship was a brilliant design and gave the raiders a huge advantage over their victims. The longship was big and strong enough to travel across open sea, but it could also operate in shallow rivers, meaning that the raiders could travel inland to raid towns and settlements on any large river. It was also a very fast-moving ship and was so good it was described as "a poem carved in wood".

When there was wind they used sails, and when there wasn't any wind the crew manoeuvred their longships by rowing them. This combination meant that whatever the weather, Viking raiders could always move quickly. They could strike at any place on a coast or river without warning and disappear just as fast, before help could arrive to fight them off.

Viking raids became more and more regular during the 10th century. Soon the Vikings didn't bother to go home for the winter months, but instead set up camps and wintered over in England before continuing raiding again the next spring. In around AD 866 Viking raiders stopped raiding long enough to launch an invasion. They captured the city of York and soon held a large section of England under their power, the Viking area being called the Danelaw.

The Vikings came from the countries we know today as Norway, Sweden and Denmark. Some Vikings were trouble-making roughnecks whose whole life was fighting and raiding. For most Vikings though, as we saw with Tor's family, raiding was an occasional summer occupation that went hand in hand with running a farm back at home.

The Vikings were amazing seafarers and explorers. As well as navigating along the coasts of Europe to the south, and Russia to the east, their ships also headed west into the North Atlantic. The Vikings discovered Iceland around AD 870, and there were soon more than 10,000 Vikings living in settlements there.

The far larger Greenland was discovered by accident when a Viking ship heading for Iceland was blown off course by storms. Greenland was explored and named by Erik the Red who hoped the name "Greenland" would make it sound a more welcoming place than the chilly sounding "Iceland" next door.

Around the year AD 1000, Erik the Red's son, Leif the Lucky, sailed still further west and became the first European to set foot in North America. They called it "Vinland" after seeing what he thought were grapes growing there. The voyage was long and dangerous though, and not many other Vikings followed him. Soon his small band of settlers had been driven out by a fatal combination of bad weather, starvation, and bow-and-arrow attacks by Native American Indians.

At the beginning of the Viking age, most Vikings followed Norse Gods like the all-wise Odin, and Thor, his giant-killing son. As the Vikings had more contact with the rest of Europe (most of which was Christian by this time) many of them began to convert to Christianity themselves. A lot of people continued to worship the old gods though, and many people did a bit of both.

Another factor in the Vikings conversion to Christianity was that they were very keen to trade with the rest of Europe and being "fellow" Christians made that easier. Viking traders carried little sets of scales with them on their travels so that items could be sold or paid for with a certain weight in silver (called "hacksilver" because it was silver hacked up, i.e. cut up). They exported furs, amber beads, whale bone, and walrus ivory from their homelands and imported things like cloth and wheat from England and wine from France. With their superior sailing skills, they were among the greatest trading people in the world.

Until relatively recently, the Vikings had quite a bad press in history books. They were often considered as noble savages and wild men intent on killing and violent raiding. Although doubtless some Vikings did fit that description, most did not. Viking seamanship was easily the finest of their time and their territories stretched as far as the shores of America. Viking craftsmanship was able to create superior swords, axes and spears, as well as beautiful jewellery like brooches, necklaces, rings, and bracelets.

There are many ways in which the legacy of the Vikings lives on around us today. Over 1,000 Viking words became part of the English language. When you use the words *get*, *give*, *both*, *knife*, *egg*, *sky*, *skin*, *again*, *birth*, *cake*, *fog*, *law*, *neck*, *sister*, *seat*, *sly* and *smile* you're using words brought to England by Viking longship.

They also gave us some of the names of the days of the week. Tyr (who had his hand bitten off by the wolf) saw his Tyr's Day become Tuesday. Odin's day became Wotan's Day or Wednesday. Thor's Day became Thursday, and Odin's wife Frigga's Day became Friday.

Perhaps the most important way that Viking culture survives today is in the saga of Odin and his fellow Norse gods. The cycle of stories begins with the birth of the world from fire and ice – two elements that would have seemed the centre of the world for Vikings living in the colder north. Odin is the leader of Asgard, and the father to Thor and several other gods. Odin is supposed to be all wise and all knowing, but of course he's not. (Or at least, not quite.)

When Odin slays a giant in battle, he sees that the giant's son is now an orphan. Feeling sorry for this normal-sized youngster, Odin takes him home to Asgard and introduces the other gods to Loki. Many of the stories that follow feature Loki causing trouble and mischief, sometimes on purpose (cutting off Sif's golden hair) and sometimes by accident (accepting a bet with a dodgy builder to get a wall repaired for free).

Loki begins the cycle of stories as a trickster who is mischievous but friendly. His relationship with the other gods goes downhill fast until he ends the saga by seeking revenge and leading the attack on Asgard during Ragnarok, the terrible "Doom of the Gods".

During the Viking age, stories were passed on orally by telling and retelling them from person to person. They were the entertainment around a camp fire or at a feast during the long, dark winter evenings. The tales of the Norse gods were not actually written down until several hundred years later, mostly by scribes on Iceland.

And there's one last, rather important thing the Vikings gave us. The Viking mid-winter festival of Yule was one of the most important festivals of the year. As Tor explained, Yule marked the shortest day in the year, which meant that from then on the days would get longer and warmer. Yule was celebrated with a feast and when it ended, people gave each other gifts, while above them Odin rode his chariot through the night sky pulled by his magical flying horse. One of Odin's many names, of course, was "long beard".

If you ever thought that Santa Claus's reindeer sleigh looked a little bit Viking, you might well be right.

Timeline

AD 787 Three Viking ships land on the south coast of England at Dorset. A Saxon tax officer attempts to question them and is killed.

AD 793 The monastery at Lindisfarne on the north-east coast of England suffers a full-scale raid. The murder of the monks at a respected seat of learning shocks Europe. This signals the beginning of Viking raids.

AD 795 First Viking attacks on Scotland and Ireland.

AD 835 Raids on England and Ireland become more regular, and for the first time Vikings establish camps and stay in England over winter.

AD 841 Vikings found the town of Dublin in Ireland as a base for future raids and trading.

AD 845 Viking chieftain, Ragnar, sails 120 ships full of Viking warriors up the river Seine to Paris, laying waste to everything in their path. They take control of the city and hold it to ransom, gaining a horde of silver for their trouble.

Circa AD 860 Lost Viking voyager, Gardar the Swede, is blown off course and discovers Iceland.

AD **866** A large army of Viking raiders invade the north of England and capture the city of York.

AD **870s** Emigration to Iceland begins with over 10,000 Vikings sailing there in the next few decades.

AD **871** Wessex gets a new ruler, King Alfred. He rules the south of England while Norsemen rule most of the north.

Circa AD **928** All good farmland on Iceland is now taken.

AD **930** Viking sailors blown off course discover Greenland. They explore a small area and return.

AD **960** Denmark adopts Christianity as the official religion, although many people continue to worship the Old Norse gods.

AD **983** Erik the Red is exiled from Iceland for murder. Exploring Greenland, he discovers the ice-free east coast and settles there.

AD **985** Bjarni Herjolfsson sails from Greenland; blown off course, he sights a large landmass to the west, but does not make landfall.

AD **1000** Iceland adopts Christianity as the official religion.

Circa AD **1001** Investigating earlier reports, Leif Eriksson, son of Erik the Red becomes the first European to set foot in America. He names it Vinland ("Land of Wine"). A small settlement is founded before they are eventually driven away by Native American Indians.

AD **1066** Harald the Ruthless and his Viking army attack the city of York, but are defeated by King Harold defending England. King Harold then marches his men south to stop William the Conqueror invading from the south coast. William is descended from Norsemen who settled in France 150 years before. William the Conqueror wins the Battle of Hastings and claims the English throne.

AD **1070s** Viking raids stop almost completely, but trading all over Europe continues. It is the end of the Viking Age.

Picture acknowledgments

P 167 Viking longhouse, Trelleborg, Denmark, CORBIS/Maurizio Gambarin.

P 167 Excavation of Oseberg longboat, 1904, AKG-Images.

P 168 Longboat Osberg, Vikinskiphuset, Oslo, CORBIS/Christophe Boisvieux.

P 169 Valhalla & the Midgard Serpent, Bridgeman Art Library London/Arni Magnusson Institute, Reykavik, Iceland.

P 170 Longboat replica, Bohuslan, Sweden, Alamy/Bjorn Svensson.

P 171 Viking re-enactment, Viking Festival at Aarhus, Denmark, C.ORBIS/Bob Krist.

P 172 "Thor hammer" pendant, Werner Forman Archive/Statens Historiska Museum, Stockholm.

P 172 Smith's mould for casting both Christian Crosses and Thor's hammers, Werner Forman Archive/National Museum, Copenhagen.

P 173 Jelling rune stone, Alamy/North Wind Picture Archives.

P 174 Map of Viking exploration routes, CORBIS/MAPS.com.

A reconstructed Viking longhouse at Trelleborg, Denmark.

A photograph of the excavation of the Oseberg longboat in Norway in 1904.

The Oseberg longboat.

Valhalla and the Midgard Serpent, from an Icelandic manuscript written around 1680.

A Swedish longboat replica.

A Viking re-enactment group at a Viking festival at Aarhus, Denmark.

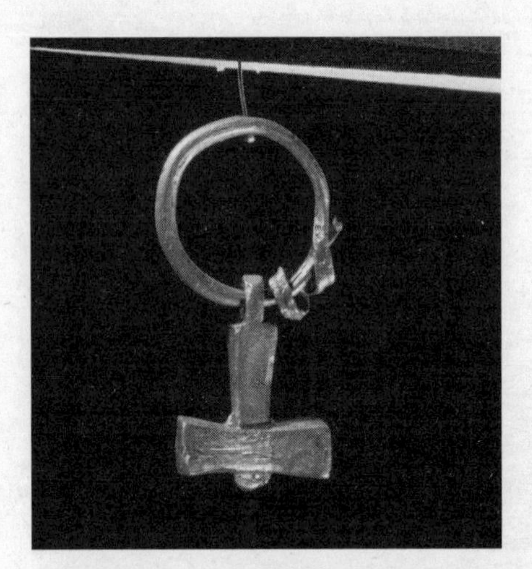

Thor's hammer pendant.

A mould for casting both Christian crosses and Thor's hammers.

A drawing of the Jelling rune stone from Jelling in Denmark.

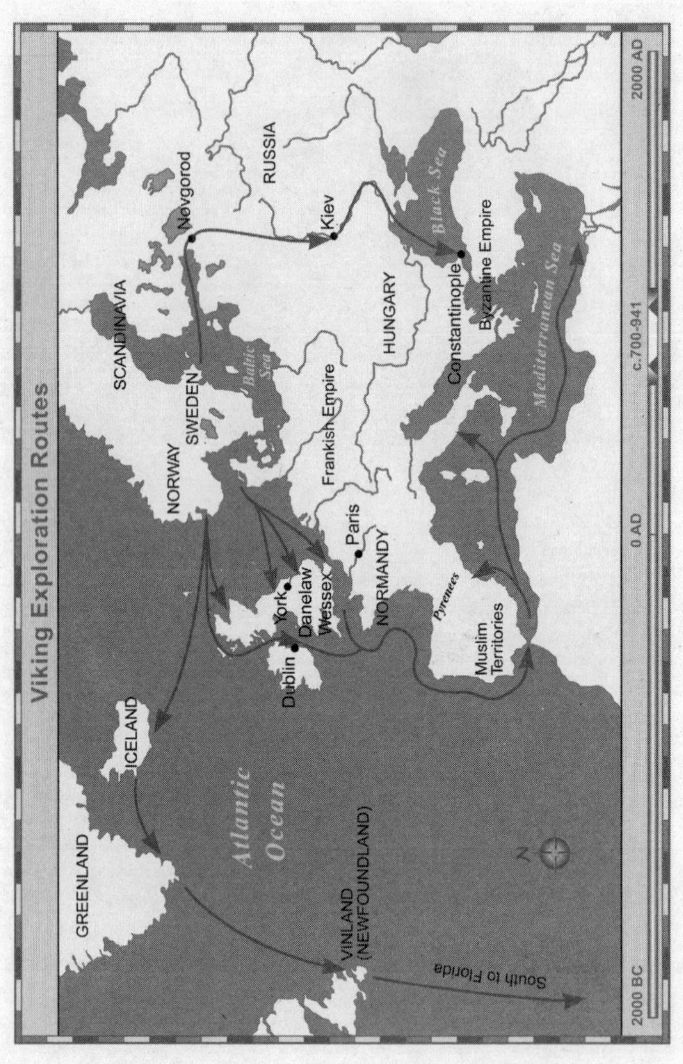

A map showing Viking exploration routes. Vikings explored as far as America (shown just off the left-hand side of the map).